UNFORGETTABLE

BOOK 1 OF THE *JOHNSON FAMILY* SERIES

DELANEY DIAMOND

CHAPTER ONE

"You can't make him love you. When the right woman comes along, he'll do all the things for her you wish he'd do for you. And do you know why? Because she's the one for him. Sorry darlin'—if he hasn't changed after three years, you're not the one."

Enthusiastic applause followed Lucas Baylor's latest advice to another woman struggling in her relationship. Seattle was the last stop on his multi-city tour to promote his book, *The Rules of Man*. Men were present, but the audience consisted mostly of women. The majority of them sought his advice, but a small percentage found his abrasive commentary appealing and were attracted to him because of it. They wanted to be the ones to tame him. While he had no intention of succumbing, he appreciated their efforts.

From the corner of his eye he saw his pregnant publicist, Brenda, in the shadows offstage, signaling he needed to wrap it up.

"We only have time for one more question," he said. A wave of groans filled the auditorium.

The moderator handed the mic to a middle-aged woman in the crowd who had no business being there with that man-hating scowl on her face. He readied himself for whatever scathing remark she would make.

"Mr. Baylor," she started, her eyes filled with anger. No doubt a man had hurt her at one time. He knew the type. "On page one-oh-five of your book, you said a man is only interested in one thing when he meets a woman. I think that's a sexist thing to say, and it's not only an insult to men by making them appear to have no depth, but it's an insult to women. We have much more to offer than our bodies. We have brains and we have feelings, Mr. Baylor. Something I wonder if you know anything about."

Catcalls, groans, and boos filled the audience.

Lucas lifted his hand to quiet them down. "Listen darlin'," he said, slathering a thick layer of Southern accent onto his words, "when a man first meets you, he's only interested in sex. He's not interested in your personality. He don't care how many degrees you have or that you're passionate about saving the whales. He don't care about none of that, because he don't know you." Chuckles of acknowledgement came from the men. "Everything he does, from opening the door to buying you dinner to pumping your gas, is an investment in time to the ultimate goal of getting in those panties."

The men in the audience barked their agreement.

"Well, what if I just want sex?" the woman demanded, lifting her chin to a defiant angle.

"Well, if that's all you want, go get it, then. Let me be the first to beat the other men in here to the punch…can I have your number?"

The crowd roared, and several of the men stood on their feet and started calling out to her. She actually blushed.

"I don't get it. Are men really that shallow?" she asked.

"Shallow has nothing to do with it. We're simple creatures. Do you want the truth or not?"

"Of course I want the truth. One of my friends—"

"Ahh, here we go. One of your friends. Let me guess, this friend is a woman, right?"

She nodded. Murmurs filled the room, and the woman looked around, her face confused. His regular fans knew he covered this topic in the book and on his blog—the danger of taking advice from other women about men instead of listening to what a man had to say for himself. She needed to hear the truth. After all, that's why she'd come to his show.

"Women need to stop listening to their girlfriends. Am I right?" Audience members nodded their heads and clapped. When he'd received enough encouragement, Lucas lifted his hand to silence his fans. "All we ever hear from women is that we don't talk and you want to know about our feelings. What are we thinking? And then we tell you what we want and think, but you don't listen. You say you want to know, but you don't, because you want to do things your way."

He walked to the edge of the stage and looked her in the eyes. "First of all, men aren't shallow. We just don't complicate every little damn thing the way women do. We need two things in life, and two things only. Notice I said need. Sure, there are other things we enjoy, but we only need two things. Write this down: sex and food. That's it. So when your man comes home from a hard day of work, don't greet him at the door whining and complaining. Meet him at the door wearing your sexiest lingerie and a pair of stilettoes so high you can barely walk in them. Give him some sex so good it blows his mind. And then fix him a damn sandwich."

The men jumped to their feet, barking and pumping their fists. A wide grin spread across Lucas's face, and he pumped his fist right along with them. The woman who had spoken out flushed bright red, probably from a combination of anger and embarrassment. He winked at her and then exited the stage.

Brenda had her hands on her hips as Lucas approached her. "I can't believe you're still reciting the same tired line. That's all men need, huh?"

"That's right. Have you learned nothing hanging with me the past few years?"

She looked heavenward and shook her head. "What am going to do with you?"

"Leave your husband and run away with me?" he asked with a wolfish grin.

"Are you going to help me raise my baby?"

"Of course."

Brenda laughed. "Coming from a man who might literally be allergic to kids, I have my doubts."

"I'll make an exception in your case." He wiggled his eyebrows.

Brenda had been an early follower of his blog, and they'd met at a meet-and-greet years ago. They'd become good friends and got along so well, he couldn't imagine having anyone else by his side during this period of success.

"Whatever." Brenda shook her head again.

"Don't act like my advice doesn't work," he said. "I helped you land your husband, didn't I?"

"You'd like to think so, but I don't play games."

"It's all games, until someone gets hurt."

Brenda cocked her head to one side. "One day you'll have to tell me who she is."

"Oh brother, here we go."

She hit him lightly on the arm. "Don't deny it, Lucas. I know there's a juicy story about a woman in your past. One day I'll get it out of you."

"There's no story, Brenda. I just happen to be a very wise man." He tapped a finger to his forehead.

"Mhmm." She looped an arm through his. "Come on, you've got at least another hour and a half of work before we can get out of here."

They'd set a table at the front of the auditorium with copies of his book. Though his blog had been popular, sales of *The Rules of Man* performed better than his publishers had anticipated. Lucas had found success by offering a mixture of shoot-from-the-hip honesty and humor that resonated with males and females around the country. His popularity gained traction from his blog, *Why He Won't Marry You*, where he gave advice to his female readers.

In addition to the table with his books, several more were covered with shirts, mugs, and other items for sale. Three young women wearing black T-shirts with *Marriage Material*—his bestselling product—written in white cursive font across their breasts manned the tables.

Lucas sat down and greeted his fans, autographing books and any other items they brought over for him to sign. By the end of the night, his cheeks ached from smiling so much, and his hand had developed a slight cramp from the number of times he'd had to write his name.

Hours later, after saying good night to Brenda, a hired car took him to the Four Seasons. The hotel sat in the heart of downtown on Union Street, within easy walking distance of the waterfront and the city's other tourist attractions.

He crossed the tiled floor of the brightly lit lobby to the bank of elevators and thought about his plans for the rest of the week. He didn't have much time to rest before his flight to California for more promotional work.

He stuck his hand in his pocket and fingered the cards slipped to him by five different women who'd attended the event. He smiled to himself. He'd call one of them tomorrow. He was too tired now. His shoulders ached and his feet hurt, but tomorrow was a new day.

The elevator doors slid open, and he stepped in. He punched the number for his floor then rested his head against the wall. He closed his eyes. A radio spot first thing in the morning, a local TV show, and then the speaking engagement had made for a long day. He couldn't wait to fall into bed.

The sound of a woman's laugh made his head snap forward. He froze as the sound carried around the corner. The familiar giggle jump-started his heart and hurtled him back in time.

The laughter reached him again, this time from farther away. At the same time, the elevator started closing and shook him out of his trance. He lunged away from the wall and shoved his hands between the doors, almost crushing his fingers in his haste.

Was his mind playing tricks on him? It couldn't be her, could it? After so much time, the sound of her laughter was so familiar, as if he'd heard it just yesterday.

Unsure of the origin of the sound, he hurried in what he thought was its general direction. His heart raced as he rounded the corner and looked wildly around the lobby. At this time of night it was almost empty. A few guests were checking in, but he knew with certainty none of them owned that voice. He rushed over to the front desk.

"Excuse me, was there another woman here just now? I think I know her."

The female clerk looked up. "Two women headed toward the front of the—"

Lucas took off before she finished, racing toward the front. He pushed through the glass doors. A family exited a taxi and two cars idled nearby. He scanned them frantically, quickly dismissing the passengers in each one.

Where was she? Had it been his imagination?

He spun in a half circle.

Just because they were in the same city didn't mean he'd run into her.

At the end of the driveway, a black sedan waited to merge into traffic. He couldn't see the occupants, but he made out the outline of two women. That had to be the car, but as he approached it took off. He sprinted after it and watched in dismay as the vehicle accelerated down Union Street.

"Hey!" he hollered. "Hey! Wait!" He waved his arms.

The tail lights grew smaller and smaller as the sedan drifted away. Panting, Lucas slowed to a stop and tried to catch his breath. What in the world had possessed him to chase after that car, as if he could catch it?

A car horn honked behind him and he jumped out of the way. He stood there, breathing heavily, watching the vehicle disappear from sight. His racing heart felt ready to burst out of his chest.

He wasn't certain she was in that car or even that the voice belonged to her. Maybe her laugh wasn't as unique as he remembered, and it *had* been nine years since he'd last heard it. Still…something inside of him said it was her. Deep in his gut, he knew.

Still slightly out of breath, Lucas trudged back to the hotel, significantly more deflated than he'd been earlier, not even sure why he'd wanted to see her so badly.

He re-entered the hotel and noticed a marquee he hadn't paid attention to before. He walked right up to the signage and read the words announcing an anniversary reception for Full Moon beer, the popular brand of beer her family brewed. It had to have been her. She must have gone there instead of outside. His heart rate tripled again.

It didn't take him long to find the ballroom and the remainder of the party. When he arrived, two empty podiums sat on either side of the open door where greeters must have stood and checked in the guests. No one stood there now; the festivities were clearly winding down. Four people sauntered out of the ballroom and a couple chatted on the outside of the door. They paid him little attention when he walked up.

Inside the room, he ambled around the perimeter, his eyes searching, his heartbeat still abnormally fast. Then he saw her.

He almost overlooked her because her shoulder length hair was much longer now. The vision in front of him stalled his footsteps and suspended his breath for an eternity. He couldn't stop staring.

It was Ivy.

CHAPTER TWO

Standing at one of the two bars in the ballroom, Lucas sipped his beer in the Pilsner glass specially designed to commemorate the anniversary celebration. His gaze swept over the room containing Seattle's finest, dripping in diamonds and wearing tuxedos and haute couture gowns. But not only Seattle's best; a national Who's Who in entertainment and captains of industry attended the party. Apparently this event was one of many celebrations throughout the year to commemorate four decades of Johnson Brewing Company beer-making.

Across the crowded room, Ivy Johnson conversed with a man whose face was vaguely familiar. Lucas thought he might be an actor but couldn't be bothered to figure out which one.

He remained fixated, the same way he'd been the first time he'd seen her back when she'd walked into the restaurant where he waited tables. He catalogued her appearance. Statuesque and tall, she looked every bit the heiress she was in a dress that cascaded to her feet and draped around her ankles in a waterfall of champagne-colored chiffon. It shimmered against the toffee color of her skin and molded to her frame. The sweetheart neckline showed off her shoulders and the graceful curve of her neck, exposed because her long hair had been swept to one side. Blonde color accentuated the fine, dark strands, and her hair fell over her right shoulder in huge, barrel-like curls.

All of a sudden she laughed, placing a hand over her full bosom as if to contain her amusement. He couldn't hear her, but his scalp tingled nonetheless as he imagined the sound. When she was especially amused, her laugh was loud, the pitch higher. *Unladylike* she used to say, covering her mouth in embarrassment. Yet he'd loved the sound of it—perhaps his favorite sound in the whole world, next to her cries of pleasure.

Damn, she was beautiful. His gut tightened. Truly beautiful in a way that made men do double takes and had women keeping an eye on her out of a combination of fear and envy. He should leave, but he couldn't right then. Not without speaking to her at least once. Some indefinable thing had pulled him to her.

Maybe he needed to see for himself if he had been wrong, and she wasn't a heartless liar, despite evidence to the contrary. Maybe because despite everything he'd accomplished and experienced in his life, a small part of him regretted his decision to leave all those years ago—nine years to be exact—and he couldn't help but wonder what could have been if he'd stayed and fought for her.

Lucas drained his glass and set it atop the bar. He fished in his pocket and pulled out a small tin of cinnamon Altoids, a healthier substitute for the cigarette habit he'd picked up in South Korea and eventually kicked upon his return. They calmed his nerves. He popped one in his mouth and chewed until it disintegrated, the heat of the cinnamon candy filling his nasal passages. Then he started walking, keeping his eyes on her the same way he'd done since he caught sight of her.

She turned suddenly, as if someone had called her name, and she waved, laughing again. Closer now, the sound gripped his abdomen like coarse talons. At the same time, she glanced in his direction and did a double take. The smile arrested on her face and was replaced by bewilderment as her lips parted.

He stopped a few feet away and immediately the scent of her perfume enveloped him. She still smelled like flowers—a light, tempting fragrance that hinted at sensuality and made it all the harder to keep his wits about him.

"Lucas?" Ivy's fingers tightened around the gold beaded clutch in her hand. The shock of seeing him sideswiped her with the impact of a truck.

"Ivy," he said in greeting, his mouth curving upward into a smile, as if they were old friends.

He spoke with a lazy drawl, the hint of Southern accent giving her name a sweet sensuality she never heard when anyone else said it. The sound filled her with memories of humid Georgia nights and long, lazy days.

Her companion excused himself with a touch to her shoulder and joined another conversation. She let him go without uttering a single word, rendered speechless by the appearance of this ghost from the past. The years had been good to him. He'd been a good-looking co-ed and had matured into an attractive man in his mid-thirties.

The beard was new, but she'd recognized him right away. Broader and thicker, he filled out his dark suit in a way that left no doubt the body underneath the expensive material was in good shape. His skin was a deep brown—mahogany—and his eyes dark and welcoming with long, curled eyelashes that would be feminine on any other man. But not on Lucas Baylor. He was all man. Six foot two inches of raw sex appeal.

An awkwardness she hadn't felt in years filled her. Were they supposed to hug? Shake hands?

"What are you doing here?" she asked.

He tucked one hand in his pants pocket and surveyed her. "I'm in Seattle on a promotional tour for my book."

She'd meant what was he doing at the party. Had he purposely avoided answering the question? "You're an author?"

He nodded. "I wrote a book called *The Rules of Man.*"

Interesting. "Congratulations."

"Thanks. Seattle's the last stop on my tour."

She felt a surge of happiness he'd achieved his heart's desire to be published. "That's wonderful. I knew you could do it." She wanted to hug him but held back, locking her hands in front of her to resist the urge.

He shrugged, as if it was no big deal. But it was. He'd always been a lover of the written word and had regaled her with original poetry and pages of lyrical prose. The simplest sentence took on a new texture and depth when he reworked it.

"You did always have nice things to say about my writing," he said, and she thought she detected a level of fondness in his voice. "So…it's been a long time."

"Nine years." She shook her head in shock. "I can't believe you're here."

He chuckled, an appealing, masculine sound that made her insides twist painfully. He seemed so relaxed, yet she was a cluster of nervous energy. She'd thought she'd matured enough to handle seeing him again should the occasion ever occur, but clearly she hadn't. Not when the sight of him was so jarring, so...debilitating.

She struggled for something to say, latching on to a neutral topic to keep from getting too personal and dredging up memories better left in the past.

"I admired everything you wrote. I could barely put two sentences together, but you, you were brilliant." She sounded like a groupie and felt a bit foolish at her gushing.

"English was always my strength, I guess. But I couldn't do what you do, messing around with statistics and projections and strategic management. All of that was, and still is, over my head."

"I didn't have much of a choice if I was going to be an active contributor in the family business." A business she'd conveniently avoided telling him about at first.

He looked around the room. "Is your husband here?"

His question surprised her. She hadn't expected him to take the conversation in that direction. "My husband passed away two years ago."

His brows lifted. "I had no idea. I'm sorry to hear that. Are you...?"

"I'm fine. It's gotten easier."

"And your daughter?"

Startled, tension coiled in her stomach and her gaze tightened on him, but he gave no indication his question was anything more than polite conversation. "She's managed well. Kids are amazingly resilient."

"Excuse me." A female voice interrupted their conversation. Ivy turned in the direction of an older couple, appreciative of the temporary respite from the conversation.

"We have to leave," the woman said. "It was lovely to see you and your brothers again."

"Thank you for coming." Ivy clasped the wife's hand and they gave each other air kisses, one on each cheek, before she and her husband walked away.

"I should go," Ivy said to Lucas. She waved her hand vaguely at the room. "We have so many guests here tonight."

"I know you're busy, but I was wondering if we—"

"I'm sorry, but I see someone I need to speak to." Her insides quivered in alarm at the suggestion he'd almost voiced. He was about to ask to keep in touch, to speak to her privately—something—and she had to avoid that.

She took him in, memorizing his face, the breadth of his broad shoulders and the beauty of his eyes. She used to tease him about the unfairness of him having such long lashes while she was stuck wearing false ones to get the same look he had naturally. "It was nice to see you again."

As she walked by him, she paused.

"How's Mama Katherine?" Lucas's mother, whom she'd called Mama Katherine at the older woman's insistence, had welcomed her into their life with open arms.

His dark brown eyes were neutral, studying her. She knew he had questions, but she was afraid of where the conversation would lead and what he would uncover.

"She passed away a few years ago."

"Lucas, no." A wave of sadness washed over her.

"Yeah, it was tough at first, but she's in a better place. She died peacefully in her sleep. All the kids came back for the funeral—everyone who could, anyway."

Mama Katherine had taken in dozens of foster children over the years. She'd had a no-nonsense attitude about her, and when Ivy had met her she'd insisted she call her Mama Katherine, like all "her kids" did. The chatter and laughter of her foster kids and children from the neighborhood always filled her house, and it wasn't unusual to find people who'd stopped by to spend time with her and soak up her wisdom.

She'd taken Lucas in when he was about fourteen years old, a troubled teen with rough edges. She'd worked on him, smoothing those edges with discipline and love and watched him graduate from college with first a bachelor's degree in creative writing and then a masters in English.

"I'm so sorry," Ivy said.

His gaze softened. "You did love her, and she loved you, too."

"I had a second mother for a short time."

Very short. Only a few months during the summer she and Lucas had spent together. When her relationship with him ended, she'd mourned the loss of her relationship with his mother almost as much.

Now she grieved again with the knowledge that someone so generous with her time and love was no longer among the living.

"Take care, Lucas."

Unable to help herself, she reached out and squeezed his arm. Feeling the muscles there, she caught her breath at the raw power emanating from him. The type of power that had kept her pinned beneath him, his heavy thrusts making her breathless, panting, pleading.

He tensed under her touch, and their gazes collided, eyes lingering a fraction too long on each other. Desire whipped through her, and her body throbbed with awareness so sudden, so basic, it frightened her.

She escaped with rapid steps across the room. She didn't want to see that look in his eyes, because then she'd be tempted to stay and talk and bask in his presence. Tempted to exchange numbers and try to recapture the magic they'd shared during their brief time together. She risked revealing too much if she did.

Resisting the urge to look back, she wondered the entire time she walked away if he was still standing there, staring after her.

Nine years ago, meeting Lucas had changed her life for good. He had no idea how much.

CHAPTER THREE

"Who was that guy?" Ivy's older brother, Cyrus Jr., frowned down at her. "I don't recognize him."

No surprise that Cyrus questioned her. His attention to detail was impeccable.

"I guess you could say he's someone from my past." She kept her voice emotionless so as not to alert her perceptive brother.

"I saw him checking you out earlier."

Her heart jumped. "You did?"

"He was watching you from the bar over there." He motioned with his chin.

"Stop frowning," she said. She wrapped her arm around his.

He wore a permanent scowl on his face. He'd taken on the responsibility of running the family business at a young age, and he took it way too seriously. A health nut and a teetotaler, Cyrus was the only one in the family who didn't drink beer, something few people outside of the family knew. He brought a glass of organic white grape juice to his lips and took a sip.

"If you keep that look on your face, people are going to think you're not having a good time," Ivy told him.

"I'm not."

She smiled, amused at his candor. Cyrus was too tactful to be so blunt when speaking to anyone else. He'd only admit something like that to her or Trenton. Speaking of which...

"Where's Trent?" She scanned the room for their younger brother.

"Probably in a closet somewhere," Cyrus said dryly.

"You're never going to let him forget that, are you?"

Several months ago Trenton had been caught with a server in a closet at a charity function. To keep the incident quiet, Cyrus had donated another $75,000 to the cause, doubling their original donation.

Her brother grunted. "If he spent half as much time working as he does chasing women..."

"Now you really sound like Number One," Ivy teased.

She and Trenton fondly called Cyrus Mr. Johnson Number Two. Their father had passed away years ago, and it had taken a long time for them to get to the point where it was no longer painful to discuss him openly.

He grunted again.

"Trent does a good job and you know it," Ivy chided, squeezing his arm.

"Think of how much more of a good job he'd do if he focused on work instead of sexual escapades."

She tended to agree with Cyrus but wouldn't admit it. Trenton was the youngest of her brothers, and while it was true he still had some growing up to do, she looked the other way at his behavior because of what he'd been through as a child.

"I'm going to head up to my condo," Ivy said. "Do you think it would be rude of me to leave right now?"

"Who in their right mind would question you?" A healthy dose of arrogance filled Cyrus's voice. He had a point. This was their event, their year.

"I'll say good-bye to a few people and then head up. Goodnight."

He nodded absentmindedly and had barely taken two steps when a guest nabbed him in conversation.

****

Ivy didn't see Lucas again, and she assumed he'd left after she'd escaped from him. She said her good-byes, left the ballroom and took the elevator up to the private residences of the hotel. At her condo she opened the door and almost immediately the sound of little slippered feet pounding on the hardwood met her ears.

"Mommy!"

Her daughter, Katie, appeared in a blur of pink and flung herself at her, wrapping her arms around Ivy's waist. She was eight years old but often mistaken for younger, her small size an oddity considering she had height on both sides of the gene pool.

Her daughter would likely go through a growth spurt, the same as she had done in middle school, when she'd shot up taller than most of the boys in her class and morphed into all arms and legs. She looked back on those years not-so-fondly and called them the Awkward Years.

She glanced down into her daughter's bespectacled face. "You're supposed to be asleep, young lady." She cupped Katie's chin.

Janelle, the babysitter, came rushing up. "I'm sorry, Ms. Johnson. I couldn't get her to go to sleep. She kept saying you should have been home by now and wouldn't go to bed until you did."

Janelle had been babysitting for Ivy the past few months. Ivy had found her through a childcare service, Nanny Services on Call, after the woman she'd been using for several years moved away. Janelle was younger, but she came highly recommended and passed all the usual background checks. Her fondness for Katie and dedication to the job were unquestionable.

"I stayed a little longer at the party than planned. Without Mother there, it was important we have a solid presence. I left Cyrus in charge now that things are dying down." Ivy pulled cash out of her purse and handed the young woman a few bills.

Janelle refused to take the money. "Ms. Johnson, you don't have to do that."

Ivy paid the service directly, but every now and again she gave Janelle a little something extra. "I insist. I want you to get that car you've been saving for." She grasped Janelle's hand and squeezed the money into it.

"Thank you so much, ma'am." Janelle smiled down at Katie. "Bye, munchkin."

"See, I told you she wouldn't be mad," Katie said.

"I'm not happy about you being up so late," Ivy said, "but I'll deal with you after Janelle leaves."

"Aww. I was just worried, Mommy. I wanted to make sure you came home safe and sound."

Every so often Katie made those types of remarks. It stemmed from the fact that Ivy's husband, Winston, had left one night and never come home. For a long time afterward, Katie had been inconsolable and clingy when it came to being separated from her mother. After Winston's death, the grave expression on her daughter's face had been heartbreaking. Better to see her in this state—happy, impish, the way an eight-year-old should be.

"Off you go. I'll be there in a minute."

Katie scurried to her room, her cat slippers making slapping sounds on the oak floors extending throughout their home. Ivy said goodnight to the babysitter and turned out the lights before going down the hall. She'd moved into the two-bedroom condo after her husband passed away. The back half contained the bedrooms, a home office, and a media room that separated her bedroom from her daughter's.

She and Winston had owned a six bedroom house, but after his death, the house had felt too large and empty. Her condo was not small by any means, however. At over four thousand square feet, the dwelling provided more than enough room for her and Katie, while giving the feel of a smaller, more intimate dwelling. The spacious living room/dining room area contained giant windows that gave an impressive view of Elliott Bay with commercial buildings in the foreground and the mountains in the background. From her bedroom she could step onto the terrace to admire the view there too, but it wasn't necessary. More than half of the bedroom's walls were floor to ceiling glass and provided a breathtaking panorama of the sun setting over the bay in the afternoons.

She'd grown to love living within the city limits for its convenience. She was close to work and within walking distance of Pike Place Market, where she and the other locals would go early in the morning to purchase fresh fruits, vegetables, fish, and deli items before the tourists showed up to explore and videotape the singing fish throwers. The Seattle Art Museum was another favorite haunt within walking distance, and when the weather was nice she and Katie went on outings at nearby Waterfront Park.

Moments later, Ivy sat on the edge of her daughter's bed, maneuvering through a negotiation about a sleepover.

"But *Mommy*, all of my friends are going."

Ivy did her best to ignore the plaintive wail of Katie's voice and the frown on her face. "You're too young for a sleepover," she said. She tucked the blanket securely around her daughter's small body.

"I'll be the only one who can't go." Katie pushed her glasses up her nose and pouted.

Ivy leaned over her on one arm. "You're too young."

Behind her glasses, Katie's eyes turned glassy and her lower lip trembled.

Ivy sighed, and sensing she was weakening, Katie went in for the kill. "*Please*, Mommy."

"Let me think about it."

Katie squealed and clapped her hands rapidly. "Yes!"

"I didn't say you could. I said I would think about it."

Ivy shot her a look, but they both knew her scowl didn't mean anything. It was a wonder her daughter wasn't spoiled. By all rights she should be a brat, with her mother being such a softie, her doting uncles and an indulgent grandmother, but she wasn't. No matter what, her daughter maintained a sweet disposition.

"Okay, I'll let you think about it," Katie agreed quickly. She clamped her mouth shut, clearly not wanting to mess up her chances.

Ivy cupped Katie's chin and looked down into the familiarity of those dark brown eyes bordered by thick, curled lashes on the top and bottom. Was she being overprotective? She brushed aside the thought. Children grew up so fast. Before long, Katie would be dating and giving her hell.

"You know I'm not doing this to be mean, but you're my baby and I need to make sure you're okay."

"I know, but I'm almost a preteen. You don't have to worry so much, and I know a lot."

"You don't know as much as you think you do, munchkin."

"You worry too much, Mommy." Sometimes she sounded so mature for her age.

"I'm your mother, and I could never worry enough, believe me." Ivy smiled. "You ready for our lunch tomorrow?" It was the last day she could fit in lunch with her daughter before school started the following week.

"Yes!" Katie's face lit up.

Ivy removed her daughter's glasses and placed them on the bedside table. She tapped her own cheek. "Give me a kiss."

Katie planted a wet one on her skin and then rolled over onto her side. "G'night."

Ivy sat there for a little longer and looked at her, her heart cheerful and sad at the same time. Her daughter was a blessing, but also a constant reminder of what she'd lost.

Right now she looked forward to a restful sleep that hopefully wouldn't include too many dreams of Lucas. She didn't want to think about him, but knew she would once she was alone with her thoughts.

"Good night," she said finally. She leaned down and kissed her daughter's soft cheek. "Love you."

"Love you, too," Katie mumbled, her voice already drowsy.

Ivy exited quietly and went to her own bedroom to undress. Seeing Lucas had her wired, and she needed to calm down. She pulled a silk kimono over her cami and matching shorts and walked back down the hallway. She peeked in on Katie and then moved to the kitchen, her tread quiet in a pair of thick socks.

Inside the pantry, she used the stepstool to reach behind the canned and boxed food to her secret stash of chocolate bars. They weren't just comfort food; she was addicted to the sweets, and tonight she needed their soothing creaminess.

She poured a healthy dose of wine into a long-stemmed glass and walked over to the window in the living room. Most of the time she kept the motorized shades up so she could enjoy the view any time of the day and night.

She sipped the rosé and bit into the candy, but the flavors didn't generate the pleasure they usually did. She found little comfort in her late night indulgence, her mind unsettled because she continued to think about Lucas.

The first time she'd seen him he'd flirted with her and her friends, and his sense of humor had piqued her interest. During the course of the meal at the restaurant where he'd worked, she'd caught him looking at her several times, and not in the way a server paid attention to a customer. He'd been interested right from the start, the same way she had been.

She'd paid the tab for the meal, and on the way to the car with her friends, she'd heard her name being called.

"Ms. Johnson! You forgot something." She'd turned and it was him, and when he caught up with them he handed her a folded piece of paper. With a sexy smile that had turned her insides mushy, he'd said, "You forgot my number. Call me," and hurried back inside.

Ivy smiled to herself, remembering his words when she finally called.

"Do you have a habit of picking up waiters in restaurants where you dine?" he'd asked.

"Yes. I have one in every city."

His amused laugh came right away. They'd made a date for when he left work the next day, and so had begun her summer romance with Lucas Baylor.

Ivy sat down on one of two sofas and picked up her electronic tablet from the table beside it. She swiped the screen and did what she'd avoided doing over the years. She did a search for Lucas and found his website.

On the home page she saw his book prominently displayed, *The Rules of Man*, dubbed the relationship handbook for the modern woman. She read the blurb and then continued to explore the site. In the bio section he gave a quick summary of his educational background and his current life.

He was an adjunct professor of creative writing at Mercer University's Atlanta campus and wrote a weekly blog. She was surprised to learn that he'd spent three years teaching English in South Korea instead of the one-year assignment he'd initially signed up for. He must have loved it there. His author website didn't mention whether or not he was married, but she hadn't seen a ring on his finger.

"Interesting name," she murmured, when she saw the blog title read *Why He Won't Marry You*.

She skimmed the articles, most of which covered what women should expect in romantic relationships, from a male perspective. Clearly he was successful based on the thousands of blog followers, and each of his posts had hundreds of commenters. Full conversations and heated debates took place in the comments section.

She zoomed in on the headshot of him and focused on the broad, megawatt smile that rivaled the brightness of the sun.

He had nice lips. She traced a finger over them and closed her eyes. A quiet shudder ran through her as she remembered how much she'd enjoyed kissing those deliciously thick lips of his.

"Luscious Lucas" her friends had called him. Every time they said it, they added a lascivious smile and a little shimmy—all because of those lips of his. And she'd been the lucky one who'd enjoyed them during the most exciting summer of her life.

Sighing, Ivy clutched the tablet to her chest.

What would he do—how would he react, if he knew what she'd done?

CHAPTER FOUR

Ivy's driver pulled up in front of the Johnson Enterprises building, the seat of her family's multi-billion dollar beer and restaurant business. The family business had started as a small brewery a generation before and blossomed into a heavyweight in the beer industry. It was one of the few beer companies still privately-owned *and* U.S.-owned. Their chain of restaurants were a successful and lucrative enterprise, as well.

She waited for Lloyd to come around and open her door.

"Don't forget to pick up Katie for my lunch with her," she said as she stepped onto the pavement.

"Only you and the little one today?" Lloyd asked.

"Yes. No executives or bankers or anyone like that." She smiled. "Just me and Katie. She's been looking forward to our lunch date, so I cleared several hours for her. Janelle will be waiting downstairs at the hotel with her for you, and you can bring her up in the executive elevator."

"Understood, ma'am. Have a good morning."

Ivy lifted her briefcase over her shoulder and walked into the atrium. Employees buzzed around and headed to their offices. Some acknowledged her with head nods. Others averted their eyes as if not worthy to even look at her. The latter response always made her uncomfortable.

"Good morning." She called the cheery greeting to the security guards posted near the elevators.

"Good morning, Ms. Johnson," they both greeted her.

"How are you?" the older one added.

"Fine." Ivy paused at the desk. "How's your grandbaby?"

His eyes lit up. "He's walking now."

"No way. Already?"

"Yes, ma'am." His face filled with pride.

"Next thing you know, he'll be pulling everything down."

He chuckled. "He's already started. Taken over the house, to hear his mother tell it."

"I remember those days. I wish her luck."

She could take the executive elevator, which required swiping a card to gain access and was used exclusively by the top executives of the company. But she preferred to come in the front and mingle with the staff. On the way up, she chatted with people in the cabin before riding to the top floor alone.

"Morning," she said to the receptionist at the front when she stepped out onto her floor. Abigail was an attractive brunette with her hair styled in a chin-length bob and a wireless headset on her head.

"Morning, Ms. Johnson."

Ivy continued to another part of the floor, which opened into an office suite where her executive assistant, Cynthia, stood waiting for her arrival. With her sparkling blue eyes, flaxen hair, and exuberant personality, she'd garnered lots of attention from the men in the office, but she was a consummate professional and one of Ivy's best friends. As soon as Cynthia saw her, she walked around her desk to offer Ivy a warm cup of coffee.

"How'd it go last night?" she asked.

"It was a long night." Ivy took the coffee and entered her office. Cynthia followed close behind.

Decorated in bright colors, the office resembled someone's home rather than the office of a corporate executive. She'd chosen the casual style on purpose, bringing in her own decorator to extend the colors from her house to this space. Deep oranges, reds, and gold filled the artwork and the pillows on the gray sofas in the sitting area. An area rug in the same bright colors held the space together.

She walked around her L-shaped desk and sat down in the executive chair. Last year she'd switched out the black one for a chocolate color. The chamois-soft leather had been a splurge she was glad she hadn't resisted. The way it cupped her derriere was like sinking onto a pillow filled with down feathers.

"But how was the party?" Cynthia cracked the blinds just enough to let in light but not so much that the sunlight would be distracting.

Ivy sipped her coffee. "Great turnout, lots of people in attendance."

She toyed with the idea of mentioning Lucas, but decided against it. Why dredge up the past more than necessary? The sight of him had made her heart race the same way it did when she went full-throttle at the maximum incline on the treadmill. That bugged her. He shouldn't have affected her so much.

She and Cynthia had been friends since their days at Emory University in Atlanta. They'd immediately bonded when they discovered they both hailed from the Northwest. Cynthia knew about Ivy's relationship with Lucas because she'd been one of the friends with her the day they'd met him at the restaurant. As the weeks wore on, she'd also teased her mercilessly when Ivy ditched her friends to spend more time with him.

"Everyone seemed to have a good time," Ivy continued. "You should have come."

"No, I couldn't. Rick's only on leave for a few more days, and I want to spend as much time with him as possible." She held up her hand. "Before you say I could have brought him with me, we wanted to spend time *alone*."

"Ooh. Does that mean you finally got laid and I can stop hearing about passion parties and the toys you bought?" Ivy rolled her eyes in fake annoyance.

Cynthia giggled, blushing. "For now. I think he's given me enough loving to last until the next time I see him." She sighed dramatically. "God, I love that man."

Cynthia and Rick were lucky to have each other, and their relationship had withstood the test of long periods apart. It only seemed to strengthen their bond when they were back together.

"You have one urgent email," Cynthia said, getting back to business. "I've already drafted a response and flagged it for you."

As the Chief Operations Officer of the JBC Restaurant Group, Ivy was in charge of both chains of restaurants—The Brew Pub and Ivy's. Because she always rode to school with her daughter in the mornings, she arrived a little later than normal. Cynthia reviewed her emails first thing and flagged any that needed her immediate attention.

"One urgent email? You mean I'll actually get some work done today?" She scooted the chair closer to the desk.

"Looks like it." Cynthia headed toward the door. "Today's your lunch with Katie, right?"

"Yes, so when she gets here just bring her in."

"Will do. It'll be nice to see the little munchkin." Katie had won over the hearts of much of the staff.

Ivy set to work, tackling the email first before turning her attention to contracts that needed to be signed and revenue reports that had to be reviewed. By lunchtime, she'd crossed a number of items off her to-do list, a minor feat in itself, considering all the calls she'd also fielded. Her goal, however, was to be finished with the major tasks of the day so she could concentrate on her daughter when she arrived for lunch.

****

In the coffee shop across the street from Johnson Enterprises, Lucas sipped a cappuccino. The steel and glass structure loomed overhead, and waves of people traveled in and out constantly.

He had a good view from his post at the bar in front of the window where pedestrians walked past. Some dressed in professional business attire, while others were of the hipster crowd with their shag haircuts and bargain thrift store clothes. He'd lost track of time while sitting there, but he'd been in the same spot for a long time, reading the paper and checking emails on his smartphone, all while debating his next move.

The Johnsons employed tens of thousands of people across the United States and around the world. Cyrus Johnson Senior had built the company from his trademark lager. One craft beer product had turned into an enterprise boasting over 30 beers, seasonal blends, and limited edition releases.

The Brew Pub served as the testing ground for new beer flavors before they hit the market at large. Ivy's was their high-end establishment, named for Cyrus Senior's only daughter. They only offered select beers from the product line there, along with old Scotch and fine wines.

He hadn't known all this when he first met Ivy. She'd kept her family background a secret. Over the years he'd analyzed and re-analyzed their relationship, and seeing her last night had him thinking even more about the past. She didn't seem upset about the way their relationship had ended and had been friendly enough.

"What the hell," he murmured to himself. He'd invite her to lunch and see what she said. He had nothing to lose, and since she'd been so cordial last night, maybe some of that friendliness would extend into today.

He dropped a ten on the table, left the café, and strode across the street.

CHAPTER FIVE

Once per week, Johnson Enterprises stocked the executive lounge with snacks, juices, and fruit. Ivy passed over those options and chose a bottled water. On the way back to her office, she had to walk through the main reception area, and when she did, her heart almost stopped.

Lucas was standing there, living up to his nickname and looking as luscious as ever. Tailored black slacks hinted at the strength of his powerful thighs, and the light blue shirt did nothing to hide his massive chest and the bulge of his muscular arms.

She smoothed a trembling hand over her outfit in an effort to maintain her composure. When he turned his head in her direction, her body tingled. His eyes drifted over her royal blue dress and the gold poodle brooch over her right breast. She was certain she looked good, but something about Lucas always made her second guess herself.

"What are you doing here?" she asked, trying to quell the ridiculous excitement bubbling up inside of her.

"I hope I'm not being presumptuous, but I thought maybe I could take you to lunch?"

He wanted to take her out? She stared at him blankly and then rapidly recovered. "I have lunch plans."

"Oh." He looked disappointed but not defeated. "Do you have a few minutes before lunch then, so we can talk?"

She considered the request. What could Lucas possibly want? She took a deep, quiet inhale. "I only have about five minutes."

"Not a problem. I won't even take that much of your time." He continued to smile, and with his Southern accent, he was downright charming. She could feel herself coming apart at the seams already.

She didn't smile back but said, "Follow me," and walked ahead of him down the corridor.

In her suite of offices, Cynthia looked up briefly from her computer. Uncertain acknowledgment appeared in her friend's eyes, but instead of staring, she politely lowered her gaze and continued typing. If she remembered who he was, Ivy knew she'd grill her later about his appearance.

They entered her office and she immediately sought refuge at her desk, standing beside it to help prop her up because even such a short time in Lucas's presence left her weak-kneed.

As he looked around, Ivy took the opportunity to observe him. Her mind immediately strayed in an inappropriate direction, imagining him naked, all brown skin and muscles under the dress shirt and pressed slacks. She imagined him over her and recalled the way he would force her to say things when they made love. It wasn't enough to control her body.

"You love this shit, don't you?" he breathed.

"Yes."

"Say it, darlin'. Let me hear you say it."

"I love this shit."

"Yeah."

He plucked a nipple between his lips and sucked as if it was his last chance to get her off.

"Your secretary looks vaguely familiar to me," Lucas said.

Ivy blinked and remembered where she was. In her office, with Lucas, with hard nipples. Thank goodness for bras with padding. She crossed one ankle over the other to silence the throbbing between her legs.

"That's Cynthia. She was still living in Atlanta when we met nine years ago."

"Ah yes, now I remember."

She needed to keep her hands busy, so she picked up the limited edition Mont Blanc pen she'd used to sign documents earlier. "So...I'm surprised to see you here."

"Yeah." He rubbed his hand across his bristled jaw, which made her wonder what those bristles would feel like if she touched them herself. Were they soft, hard, somewhere in between? "I couldn't leave without coming by and saying hello. We didn't get a chance to speak last night because you were so busy."

"I'm busy today, too."

"I'm sure you are." He either didn't take the hint or didn't care. He turned in a half circle, his eyes sweeping the room. "It's strange seeing you in these surroundings, looking like an executive, so different from when I last saw you."

"I was twenty-two years old then. I was different. We both were."

"And I didn't know who you were at first," he said thoughtfully. "I never understood why you didn't tell me right away."

"For the same reason I kept it a secret from everyone. People behave differently when they find out you have money."

"Did I act like I cared?"

"No, you didn't." Which had been a pleasant surprise, making her love him even more. She glanced at his hand. "You never married?"

"No. Marriage isn't in the cards for me. You know that."

She hadn't forgotten. He'd broken her heart when he'd told her the truth about their relationship. *This isn't a forever thing. It's just a for now thing. I have plans.*

"True." Fatherhood hadn't been in the cards for him, either, but that didn't stop her from fantasizing, wishing she could have been the woman to make him change his ways. To extinguish the wanderlust that had driven him to seek adventure on the other side of the world. To make him want to settle down and start a family.

"I promised not to keep you, so I'm going cut to the chase." He tucked a hand in the pocket of his trousers. "I know the way things ended between us years ago wasn't the best, but I was wondering if we could keep in touch. The truth is, Ivy, I've never forgotten about you, and I thought maybe we could…be friends at least."

Friends.

To hide the sudden pain from his suggestion at the inadequate substitute, she looked down at the pen in her hand. There were so many reasons why she couldn't be friends with him, none of which she could share. She couldn't tell him that even though the longing had subsided over the years, she'd never stopped thinking about him. She couldn't tell him that he had a daughter—not after he'd told her he didn't want to be a father. Not after she'd lied and told him she'd taken measures to make sure she didn't get pregnant.

"Atlanta was a long time ago. I've moved on." She filled her voice with a coolness she didn't feel, hoping the same sentiment was reflected in her eyes and would fool him into walking out without a backward glance. "I was happily married for seven years before my husband passed away, and I think it's best that we keep the past in the past."

Her words swept the friendly expression from his face. "I know we've both changed a lot, and I'm not asking to revisit the past," he said. "All I'm asking is—"

"You're asking for something I can't give. I've moved on," she said in a firmer voice.

Her reaction confused him. She could see it in his eyes. "So you can't see your way to be friends?" He laughed softly, as if the idea of not accepting his offer of friendship was preposterous.

"I have plenty of friends. I don't need anymore."

"You're serious?"

"You sound surprised."

He studied her. "Maybe we should try this again."

He stalked toward her, his footfalls silent on the carpet. She stiffened at his closeness and fought to breathe normally. Surely she could handle being this close to him, even though she could smell his cologne, even though she could reach out and touch him if she wanted to.

He looked her right in the eye, and she held her gaze steady.

She was almost as tall as him in her heels. Five feet eight and a half inches, but she rounded up to five-nine, because what was a half-inch more? He used to tease her about that. He always teased her about one thing or another—her picky eating habits, her prissiness.

"Did I do something to upset you?" he asked.

"What makes you say that?"

"Because I have the distinct impression you don't want me here." He examined her face. "Am I right? You don't want me here?"

She set the pen on the desk with a measured motion and lifted her gaze to his. "I don't understand why you want to be here or what your expectations are."

"I don't expect anything. I don't want anything," he said.

"Except to be friends," she clarified.

"Yes."

"Good, we understand each other." She exhaled a deep breath.

"You want to be friends, but I don't."

He frowned. His dark, contemplative gaze searched her face. "Why?"

"I told you, I have plenty of friends already."

"If this is about the way our relationship ended, you knew the deal when we got involved. I never lied to you. It doesn't make sense that you'd still hold a grudge after nine years."

He was right. He'd been up front from the beginning, making it clear that their relationship was a summer fling and nothing more because he had big plans that didn't involve a silly socialite falling for him.

"I'm not holding a grudge. I don't want to be friends with you."

He turned away. "This was obviously a waste of time," he muttered.

"Obviously." She only had to maintain this arctic front a little longer so she could get him out of there, and then she could relax.

He swung around. "I came to talk, to see if we could build a bridge or something." Her silence fueled his anger. "For the record, I wanted to be friends, nothing more. I have plenty of women in my life."

The words had been thrust at her with dagger-like force, making it clear he didn't want *her*, no matter what she thought. Somehow she managed not to flinch.

"Good for you. Then why are you here?" she shot back.

"I'm beginning to wonder the same thing."

Right then, the door swung open and Katie bounded in, her long braids pulled back into a ponytail. Her mouth fell open and she looked up at them in surprise.

"Oops! Sorry. I didn't know you were in a meeting. Cynthia wasn't at her desk."

Ivy's kept her voice calm even though her pulse started to race. "Go back down the hall to the visitor's office. I'll be there as soon as I wrap this up."

Quietly, Katie obeyed and left, shutting the door behind her.

"She looks just like you," Lucas said. He paused. He looked at her strangely, studying her face again.

"I have a million things to do. I need you to leave," Ivy said.

His head jerked back at her abrupt dismissal. "Damn, Ivy, I just—" He shook his head. "You know what, forget it. Lucas Baylor doesn't stay where he's not wanted. Take care of yourself."

He stormed out, and after he left, Ivy closed her eyes and sagged against the desk. That was close.

CHAPTER SIX

Lucas marched down the hall, fury and the stirring of blood in his loins making his stride heavy.

What a waste of time and how embarrassing. So what they couldn't be friends?

He had plenty of friends, just like she did. So what if his eyes had dropped to the sway of her hips when she walked ahead of him? He barely even noticed that her body was rounder, fuller, more womanly.

He wanted to wrench the mask of stoicism from her lovely face. The woman he remembered had been passionate, not cool and detached. Was the old Ivy completely gone? The wild child—more child than wild—with her contradictory innocence and adventurous spirit, determined to live life to the fullest while shunning the spotlight that had dogged her for years.

He frowned.

And what had that look been about at the end? It wasn't just surprise. It was worry. No. Concern? No. *Alarm.* Why would Ivy be alarmed in his presence?

It was around lunchtime and the offices on either side of the hallway were empty. A movement in one of them caught his eye. Ivy's daughter was in there, seated in a guest chair and writing in a composition notebook on her lap.

Before he had time to contemplate his actions, he entered the office. She was part of Ivy, and that drew him out of curiosity, if nothing else.

"Hey there."

She quickly covered the pages of the book protectively with her arm.

"What do you have there?" he asked.

"Nothing." Her glasses gave her a studious, serious appearance.

"Looked like you might be working on a story," he said.

She shrugged and kept her arm over the book.

He almost smiled. He knew what it was like to want to protect your words before allowing anyone to see them and criticize. "You don't want me to see?"

She shrugged again. "I don't know if I'm any good," she mumbled.

"Any good at what?"

"Writing." Behind the black-framed glasses, she had pretty eyes, with long, curled lashes. "Writing is my hobby, and I love it. My mom says I'm like my dad in that way."

Ivy's husband had been fond of writing. That was a surprise. "So your dad liked to write too, huh?"

The little girl nodded. "Mommy said his words were like magic."

A stab of jealousy passed through him. She used to say the same about his writing. He crouched in front of her daughter. "Guess what? I'm a writer, too."

Impressed, her eyes widened. "You are?"

"Yes. Do you know what a blog is?"

She nodded.

"Well, I write a successful blog and I just had my first book published. That's why I'm in Seattle. I'm on a tour to promote it."

"Congratulations on your book. That's quite an accomplishment." She sounded intelligent and way too mature for her age. He stifled a smile.

"So what are you working on?" Lucas asked.

"Well...it's not a story or anything. It's my feelings. Just things I'm thinking about." Her voice and eyes lowered at the end and she suddenly became bashful. "But I write stories, too."

"What kind of stories?"

"Fairy tales, about a princess and a handsome prince."

"And how do those stories end?" he asked.

Her eyes lit up. "They get married and have lots of babies."

Lucas hid his amusement at her animated expression. "After they finish school, right?"

"Of course," she said solemnly.

He rose from the crouched position and looked down at her upturned face. She was a cute little replica of her mother, with the same complexion and a pair of sparkling brown eyes. She'd only been briefly mentioned in an article he'd read online about Ivy about how she managed her career as an executive while being a mother. There hadn't been a single photo of her daughter anywhere, though. Ivy had done a good job of keeping her out of the media spotlight.

"It was nice talking to you," Lucas said. He suddenly realized he didn't know her name. "What's your name, darlin'?"

"Katie. Well, it's actually Katherine, but everybody calls me Katie."

"That's a pretty name. My mother's name is Katherine, too."

"It is?"

"Sure is. Well, it was nice to meet you, Katie." He paused, struck by a random thought. Katherine? Why would Ivy give her daughter his mother's name?

Probably just a coincidence. After all, his mother and Ivy had been close during the time she and he were involved, and he could tell his mother had been disappointed when their relationship had ended. Maybe Ivy just liked the name Katherine.

His brow furrowed. Surely it was also a coincidence that Katie happened to enjoy writing, like he did.

Writing is my hobby, and I love it. My mom said I'm like my dad in that way.

Mommy said his words were like magic.

Holy shit.

"Mister, are you okay?"

Sweat broke out on his forehead and he swiped it away. He looked more closely at Katie and noticed things he hadn't before. He couldn't honestly say he saw a resemblance to him in her face. She resembled her mother, but where Ivy had a rounded tip to her nose, Katie's was flatter and broader, similar to his. And her eyelashes reminded him of his own.

No big deal. Lots of people had broad noses and long lashes, right?

He swallowed. He couldn't shake his crazy idea. It took root and germinated.

Could she be his daughter? Was that why he felt inexplicably drawn to her?

No, none of his musings made sense. He shook his head. Katie was too young, clearly only about six or seven years old. He and Ivy would have been broken up long before her conception. She would have been happily married to Winston Whats-His-Face during the time Katie was conceived.

"Yes, I'm fine," he said, his voice thick, his mind still racing. "How old are you, Katie?" he asked.

"I turned eight in April, but I can't wait until I turn nine, because my Uncle Cyrus said he's going to buy me a gold-plated cell phone. Mommy says I'm too young, but Uncle Cyrus says all the kids have cell phones, so why shouldn't I. My mom worries a lot."

He barely heard the last part of what she said. His brain quickly did the math. If her birthday was in April, that meant Ivy had probably gotten pregnant the summer they'd spent together.

The direction of his thoughts sent his mind reeling. His heartbeat tripled, the pounding echoing in his head. He recalled a broken condom, his panic, and her promise to take the morning after pill. They'd had an agreement. Surely she would have told him if she was pregnant.

He spun around when he heard a soft noise behind him. Ivy stood in the doorway, her eyes wide with apprehension.

"Mommy, Mr., um, I don't know his name, but he's a writer, too—"

"Go to my office and wait for me in there, please," Ivy said, her voice tight.

"Okay." Katie picked up her pencil and notebook. She paused at the door. "Bye, mister."

She slipped from the room and Ivy and Lucas stared at each other in silence. He was still processing his thoughts.

"I thought you'd gone." Underneath the stiff tone, there was an odd note to her voice—a sort of breathlessness.

"I'm still here." He watched her closely. "Getting to know Katherine."

He didn't hear her indrawn breath, but he saw the way her chest hitched. He stepped closer.

"Funny how you gave her the same name as my mother."

"You think so? I've always loved the name Katherine." She tried to appear calm but didn't quite pull it off. Not when the pulse at her throat was beating out of control.

"And she loves to write, just like her father. Isn't that something?"

She licked her lips. "Nothing special about it. Lots of kids take after their parents. Some children develop a love of sports. She happens to love writing."

"What did your husband write?"

"A lot of things. A little bit of this and that." She obviously couldn't think of a lie fast enough.

"Interesting." Lucas slowly rubbed his jaw. "You know what else is interesting? She told me she's eight years old."

Raw panic flashed in her eyes. Bolstered with confidence, Lucas continued. "She said her birthday's in April," he said through gritted teeth. Anger and disbelief billowed in his blood. "Isn't that interesting?"

There was no mistaking the anxiety in Ivy's face.

"I don't know why her birthday would be interesting." She glanced at the gold and diamond encrusted Cartier watch on her wrist. "You know what, I better go. As I mentioned, I have a lunch date."

"Not so fast!" She half-turned when his voice whipped out to stop her.

Lucas slammed the door shut before she could escape and moved into her personal space, so close he saw the different colors in her pupils—a dark chestnut and a smattering of lighter brown specks.

"Counting backward nine months—"

"Whatever it is you're thinking—"

"Look me in the eye and tell me I'm wrong, Ivy," he snarled. "Tell me!"

She pressed back into the wall and a trembling overtook her shoulders. He moved closer, crowding her.

"Tell me the truth," Lucas said, clenching his fingers into tightly balled fists. "Tell me the truth, goddammit!" His voice had risen louder and his words came out harsher than he'd intended, but he couldn't suppress the emotion overtaking him.

Ivy shook her head slowly, but she didn't respond. She didn't have to, because he saw the answer in her eyes.

"Jesus," Lucas muttered, taking two steps back. His legs became unsteady, and his heart thundered beneath his ribs. "Ivy..." He swallowed, at a loss for words and overwhelmed by the burning in his chest that made it hard to breathe. "She's my daughter, isn't she?"

She placed trembling fingers over her mouth. Her brows knitted together and her eyes filled with tears. She lowered her lids and drew some inner strength, because when she opened her eyes again, she appeared calmer.

"Yes."

CHAPTER SEVEN

Blood pounded in his ears. "You lied to me."

"I didn't lie to you."

"We had an agreement," Lucas reminded her, his voice a harsh whisper. "When the condom broke, we agreed you'd take the morning after pill to prevent getting pregnant. You *told* me you had taken it."

"I didn't tell you I took it."

"Are you calling me a liar?" he demanded. "I specifically remember asking you if you'd bought the pill and taken it."

"And I said don't worry, everything's taken care of," she said quietly.

He paused, scouring his memory to recall what exactly they'd said to each other. He'd been blunt and honest, just like in the beginning. He'd reminded her that soon he would be flying off to South Korea for a year to teach English. The last thing he had needed was to become a father. Fatherhood had never been an option for him, and he'd told her as much.

He'd specifically asked her if she'd taken the pill, and she'd said...now he couldn't remember. As he reflected on the conversation, she hadn't actually said yes, had she? He'd made the assumption based on her vague answer.

"So you lied by omission," he bit out.

She took a deep breath. "I told you what you wanted to hear, but I decided to let nature take its course. I decided that if I got pregnant, I would live with the consequences." She lifted her chin in a display of defiance.

"I can't believe this." Lucas paced away from her and clutched his head in his hands. Outside the window was a bright, sunny day. Inside the room, he suffocated under a cloud of disbelief. Was this really happening? "What are we going to do?"

"I don't understand."

He whirled around to face her again, and she actually looked confused.

"I'm her father," he explained, as if it needed explaining.

"As far as she's concerned, her father is dead. I don't want or need anything from you. You're free to go."

"Free to—" He broke off with a grim laugh.

"You could leave, and no one would blame you."

"You expect me to just walk away?"

"She'll never know. I haven't said a word to her about you."

Lucas fell silent as the thought took root. "So you expect me to fly out of here tomorrow and pretend I don't have a child—someone walking around in the world whose life I helped create? Half my personality, half my traits."

"You don't have to do anything if you don't want to," Ivy said. The emotion from a few minutes ago had completely dissipated. The mask was back in place and she was once again her cool and collected self. "I don't need anything from you."

"I know you don't need anything from me, princess, but this isn't about you, is it?"

Use of the endearment took them both by surprise. She stiffened and he wished he could take back the word. He'd nicknamed her "princess" almost from the moment they met, only finding out later how close to the truth he'd been. From the beginning he could tell she came from money, but when she'd disclosed the extent of her family's wealth, he'd been floored. Princess indeed, and he couldn't help but wonder why this woman would be messing around with a lowly waiter.

"You should have told me," Lucas said.

She swallowed. "You said you didn't want children. You made that very clear. You were leaving for Asia and wanted to see the world. Those were your words."

"I tell you I don't want kids, and you use that as an excuse not to tell me I have a daughter?"

"I took you at your word."

"So it's my fault you didn't tell me? Don't blame your deception on me, because the bottom line is, we had an agreement. I told you I didn't want kids, and I meant it. You had no right to 'let nature take its course.'"

"It was *my* choice."

"Yeah, your body, your choice," Lucas said in a derisive tone. "Just leave me out of it. It's only my sperm."

"I never said that."

"You don't have to," Lucas shot back. "You're not the only one who has reproductive rights."

"I'm trying to get you to understand why I never told you about her. First of all, I didn't even know how to get in touch with you."

"Give me a break. I don't believe you for one second." Lucas twisted away from her and ran his hand over the back of his head.

"How was I supposed to get in touch with you?"

He swung around. "Oh, I don't know, your family's worth billions. I'm sure you could have found a way. Hell, you could've called Mama Katherine. Admit it, Ivy. You didn't tell me because you didn't want me to know. Having me in your life didn't fit into your plans." He closed his mind to the memory of the magazine article he'd seen, celebrating her engagement to her high school sweetheart. According to the story, they'd been secretly engaged all along. The article had gutted him.

"And for some reason, your fiancé went along with this…this farce," he continued, bitterness brimming in his gut. "He was either a good man, or a fool so in love with you it didn't matter. Makes me wonder if you did tell him." His gaze sharpened, examining her face closely.

"He knew before we got married," she said.

The plot thickened. "*He knew?* And he just loved you so much he went along with it?" he asked savagely, deep down sympathizing with the sap because he had also been wrapped around her finger.

When she spoke again, her voice was softer. "The choice I made was mine."

"The choice was yours to make, but it didn't only affect you. And he had no problem raising another man's child and giving her his name?"

Ivy crossed her arms over her chest. "My relationship with

Winston is really none of your business. We had a very good relationship; our marriage worked for us." She took a fortifying breath. "I didn't think you'd want her."

She twisted the ring on her right hand, a habit he'd noticed she engaged in whenever she was uncomfortable. The ring was an antique, made of gold and set with turquoise and white seed pearls. She wore the simple jewelry as proudly as she did her diamonds because it had been passed down to her from her grandmother.

"Who else knows that Winston wasn't her father?"

She twisted the ring even faster. "Everyone. Both his family and mine."

Lucas's mouth fell open. This story got better and better. "Un-fucking-believable. Let me get this straight, all of you planned to keep this a secret? For how long?"

"I don't know. I suppose...indefinitely." He saw the guilt in her eyes, perhaps even a bit of shame at what she'd done. She should be ashamed. "What do you want to do?"

"I don't want to be a father," he grated.

He never had. He'd been cautious all along, always using condoms and had even played around with the idea of a vasectomy. Only the finality of the procedure had kept him from having the surgery. Because even though he knew without a doubt he didn't want the trappings of fatherhood, part of him held out just in case he ever changed his mind.

"Then don't be a father," Ivy said evenly.

"We crossed that bridge eight years ago."

"I said you could walk away and no one will blame you. She doesn't know you, and as far as she's concerned, her father is dead. You can go back to Atlanta with a clear conscience."

He stilled. "Is that what you want?"

"I want you to have what you want. Our lives don't have to be disrupted and neither does yours."

She was giving him a way out—freedom. Freedom from responsibility, freedom to continue his life in the way he had been living it without interruption. The travel, the women, his work—everything would remain the same. Yet he hesitated to seize the opportunity she offered.

"I could just walk out of here?"

"Free and clear." Same cool voice, same impassive features. He couldn't read her at all.

"I didn't want this, Ivy."

"You think I don't know that?" A quivering smile crossed her lips. "I understand and I don't blame you. You can make your choice the same way I did. What do you want to do?"

The same question again.

He thought about the little girl he'd just spent a few moments with. He didn't know her and she didn't know him. He could leave and she wouldn't know the difference because she already thought another man was her father. He'd just be some random guy that she'd met and would soon forget.

Instead of the excitement he would have expected, the thought knocked the wind from him. He sank onto the edge of the desk and stared at his shoes. His lungs didn't seem capable of providing enough oxygen. He gulped air into his nostrils, finding it hard to breathe all of a sudden.

"What do you want to do?" Ivy asked again.

His head snapped up. "Can't wait to get rid of me?" he asked in a biting voice.

"Like I told you before, I have lunch plans."

"Well I wouldn't want to disrupt your goddamn lunch plans. You must be fucking starving."

She flinched at his tone.

There was nothing more to say. "You want me to leave, Ivy, I'll leave." A huge knot settled in his stomach. Why didn't he feel better about this decision?

"I never said I wanted you to leave, but you can." She held her body rigid. "And I'd understand."

Their gazes locked on each other.

Still he didn't move. He could walk out and be a free man, or stay. This should be an easy decision, but it was turning out to be much harder than expected. He thought again about Katie. She had uncles, grandparents, and billions of dollars. Anything she wanted she could have, including a gold-plated cell phone when she turned nine years old. She didn't need him. He had nothing to offer. He didn't come from money, and he didn't know who he was or where he came from.

He bolted from the desk. He had to get away before he suffocated. He swung the door open and without looking at Ivy again, walked out the door.

Ivy watched him leave, and when she was certain he was gone for good, she collapsed onto one of the chairs. Not telling him had been the right decision years ago, but knowing didn't make her feel any better. In fact, his departure hurt—a deep, unexpected pain that cut through to the marrow of her bones. He'd rejected Katie, just as she'd known he would. She'd hoped, for one moment, that he would prove her wrong. Not for her, but for their daughter.

She inhaled a tremulous breath and shook off her despondency. After struggling to her feet, she walked briskly down the hallway.

He wouldn't know the wonderful human being Katie was or the intelligent, lovely young woman Ivy was certain she'd become. His loss.

She entered her office and caught her daughter spinning around in a circle in her executive chair. Ivy had told her not to do that on countless occasions.

Busted, Katie stopped and a guilty smile crossed her face. "Sorry, Mommy."

Ivy didn't have the energy or desire to scold her. Looking at her sweet face saddened her and made her heart ache.

Katie's brow wrinkled. "Mommy, is something wrong?"

Ivy shook her head, biting her lip to keep it from trembling. "Time for our lunch date. Let's go." She held out her hand and Katie ran over.

"Good. I'm hungry!" her daughter said with dramatic flair.

Ivy grinned down at her. She'd brought so much joy into her life. Not only hers, the entire family. Katie had been their savior. Losing Lucas and then her beloved father soon after had plunged Ivy into depression. The only joy in her life had been the pending birth of her daughter. After Katie was born, there had been times when she didn't want to get out of bed, but she did. Taking care of her daughter eased the pain and patched—if not repaired—her broken heart.

Even her mother, who'd been confined to bed after losing her life partner, had slowly begun to live again when Ivy had brought her newborn grandchild to her room. Katie had, miraculously, saved her fractured family. Lucas had no idea what he was missing.

"You're always hungry," Ivy teased. "Where does it all go?"

"In my tummy!" Katie rubbed her stomach and made a chomping sound.

They laughed as they started down the hall. As they passed the office where she and Lucas had talked, Katie peeked in. "Is the man gone?"

Ivy's fingers closed just a little bit tighter around her daughter's hand. "Yes, he's gone. We won't be seeing him again."

CHAPTER EIGHT

Seated at the boarding gate in Los Angeles International Airport, Lucas swallowed the last of his sandwich and crumpled the wrapper. After he'd left Seattle, he'd flown to LA for three days of radio spots, a newspaper interview, and a photo shoot for a regional magazine. The fatigue was starting to catch up with him. He felt it more often lately.

"You're not as young as you used to be," he told himself.

He licked a drop of mustard off his finger and caught the faint smile the woman in the chair across from him sent his way. He smiled in return, but looked away.

Not today, sweetheart.

He couldn't even think about hooking up with anyone right now, and it was all Ivy's fault.

Because of her, he was a father. He had no idea how to be one, didn't have one and didn't want to be one. He'd taken great pains to avoid fatherhood, and part of him was still stunned by the realization that he'd been hit by the bullet he thought he'd dodged all of his life.

How could she not tell him? And now he was supposed to drop everything and become the father he never wanted to be in the first place?

His thoughts were all jumbled because actually, she'd said the exact opposite. She'd let him off the hook and taken the news quite well that he didn't want to take on his parental responsibilities.

He rested his elbows on his knees and scrubbed his hands over his face. He had a foster family, five brothers and sisters he'd grown up with in Mama Katherine's house, but otherwise, he had no known blood relatives. Mama Katherine had told him he may not know who he was or where he came from, but that didn't make him a nobody. But when he compared his life to Ivy's, he came up short. She knew her heritage. She could trace her lineage.

The only memory he had, faint though it was, was of a woman with a large Afro leaning over him and singing the lullaby "Rock-a-Bye-Baby." He wondered if it was real or a false memory. It could be a dream, but he could almost swear his smile mirrored the one she wore as she sang to him.

The social workers had told him there was no way he could remember any such occurrence because he'd been so young when they found him, but he held on to the memory nonetheless. It was a connection to his past, no matter how fragile.

The image of her face was fuzzy and its clarity remained just out of focus. Yet he wanted to believe she was his mother. It gave him something to hold on to, no matter how small, no matter how unlikely. His throat tightened painfully, as if someone had closed their hand around his neck and he straightened in the chair, fighting the suffocating sensation. He hated the drowning feeling that sometimes came over him—as if he were tossed into the abyss and told to sink or swim.

He'd felt this way all of his life, along with a restless emptiness, not unlike being out to sea in a small vessel without a paddle or motor to propel him along. Just...drifting, without purpose or direction.

He thought again about Katie, his own flesh and blood. They shared similar traits. She liked to write just like him. Imagine that.

With a wry smile, Lucas surveyed the bustling crowd at the airport.

His foot bounced up and down as he thought.

Maybe he could do it. Maybe he could do the father-thing. The more he thought about it, the less crazy the idea seemed.

Katie didn't have a father right now. Why couldn't it be him? After all, he actually was her father.

Ivy had obviously wanted to get rid of him. She'd made it ridiculously easy for him to walk away, but he'd show her he was not so easy to get rid of.

His jaw hardened with resolve and he picked up his carry-on bag from the floor. He walked up to the ticket counter.

"I need to change my flight," he said to the airline agent. "I need your first flight to Seattle."

****

Lucas paced the atrium of Johnson Enterprises. He made the same loop over and over, from one wall to the next. The guards at the desk eyed him the entire time, as if they'd be ready to tackle him if he made a questionable move.

In the nick of time he'd been able to make the next flight out of LA. He'd had to run through the airport with energy he probably hadn't expelled since he was a teenager, but he'd made it to the gate on time. And now he was here, waiting for Ivy.

Since five o'clock, employees had been pouring out of the elevators into the atrium. Each time he searched the faces for her, and each time he was disappointed, but prepared to wait as long as it took for her to come down.

The doors purred open again and released another group of employees. Ivy was among them, and the minute he saw her his pulse rate accelerated. It was a reaction he couldn't quash, much to his chagrin.

As usual she looked amazing in a form-fitting suit. Her hair was pulled back into a loose, side-swept chignon that allowed wisps of hair to brush her right cheek like dark strands of spun silk. She waved at the guards and stopped to speak to them. While they had her attention he made his way toward her. By the time she turned around, he was almost beside her.

Her eyes widened in surprise. "What are you doing here? I thought you'd left."

"I did, but we need to talk."

"What else is there to talk about?"

"Katherine."

She eyed him with trepidation. "What about her?"

"Can we go somewhere to talk privately?" Lucas asked in a lowered voice.

He didn't want to have this conversation at the guard desk. The older guy especially was giving him the evil eye. If Ivy gave any indication that Lucas upset her, these guys looked like they'd gladly beat him down with their batons.

She didn't answer right away, but she did step away from the desk.

"I don't understand what's going on. I thought you were on your way back to Atlanta."

"I had a short trip to California and then I was headed back, but I changed my mind."

"And you want to talk?" She sounded skeptical.

"Yes. Preferably now," he said with insistence.

Her eyes clouded with uncertainty. "My driver's outside. We could go to the lounge at the Four Seasons and have a drink. It's usually quiet there this time of the day."

"Afraid to be alone with me in private?" he asked.

"Forgive me if I don't think that's a good idea. You look like you want to choke the life out of me, and I'm not ready to die yet." A vinegar smile crossed her lips, yet she still managed to look appealing.

She always did have a sarcastic sense of humor. If he weren't so unhappy about their circumstances he would crack a smile.

They walked toward the door, and he placed his hand at the small of her back. The movement was automatic, one he didn't think about until the exact moment his hand touched the base of her spine.

She jerked away from him. The abrupt motion sent her smack dab into a man walking nearby. Lucas stopped in his tracks and heard her murmur an apology to the man who smiled off the collision.

When she looked at him again, her eyes held a wildness that betrayed the cool expression on her face. "Could you try not to touch me, please," she said.

The verbal slap stung. "My mistake," he bit out. He waved his hand with a flourish. "Carry on, princess."

"Stop calling me that," she snapped.

"Why? You used to like it." He was purposely goading her, trying to get a reaction. Maybe because his insides were an emotional jumble and her impassive face, proof she had way more control than he did, struck a nerve.

"Princesses get whatever they want. I do not." She spun on her heel and marched toward the exit with more speed in her steps.

He stared after her. What the hell did that mean?

The ride to the hotel didn't take long, but the entire time Ivy stayed on the phone in an obvious effort to ignore him. Well, he wasn't going anywhere.

When they entered the hotel lounge the hostess practically tripped over herself to accommodate them. Everything was Ms. Johnson-this and Ms. Johnson-that. He was pretty sure if they hadn't had a free table for them to sit at, the young woman would have gone down on all fours and let Ivy perch on her back. Fortunately, that wasn't necessary. She wiped down a table in a quiet corner and they sat in soft-cushioned chairs across from each other.

Ivy crossed her long legs and set her gold Hermès bag on the low table between them. It seemed his senses were more heightened because her perfume enveloped him with a new scent, and it made his blood pressure spike.

"Can I get you a drink?" she asked.

"I don't want a damn drink," he replied, angry at her and at himself for the trajectory of his thoughts. Considering her deception, he was disgusted with himself for noticing anything about her.

She raised an eyebrow, surprised by his outburst. "I hope you don't mind if I have one, then," she said, lifting her hand to get the waiter's attention. She was way too calm. He wanted to unravel her.

As she discussed the wine selection with the waiter, she leaned toward the young man. She uncrossed and re-crossed her legs as they talked, and Lucas wondered if she was doing it on purpose to drive him out of his mind.

Could you try not to touch me, please.

He tossed several Altoids into his mouth and chewed them with a vengeance. Those words made him want to touch her all the more. He'd start with those long legs of hers. He recalled how they felt cinched around his waist, and his groin tightened from the mere thought. Then he'd yank the pins out of that skein of hair so he could run his fingers through her long tresses.

He'd then focus on her moist lips. She knew how to use them, that's for sure. She could suck the skin off—

Jeez. He ran a hand over his head and shifted in the chair. The woman still had him by the balls. He wanted to smash something. Maybe the vase on the table next to him. Or better yet, the table.

"And you, sir, what can I get for you?" the waiter asked with a pleasant smile.

"He's not—"

"Vodka. Straight." He pulled out his wallet and handed the young man a credit card. He had a feeling he'd need more than one drink. "Start a tab."

The waiter walked away with the card in hand.

"You didn't have to do that. I can get my own drinks."

"I know you can, and get mine, too. But I'm a Southern man, and I won't dine with a lady and have her pay for me. Nor will I allow her to pay for herself."

"You're still touting those old-fashioned ideas, Lucas?" she asked, smoothing the lines of her skirt. His eyes followed the movement. Even her knees were cute. He imagined pulling them apart and kissing her skin—from her knees up the silken length of her thigh to...heaven.

Lucas shifted again and searched for the waiter. Where the hell was he with that drink?

"Your ideas are outdated in today's society," Ivy said.

He returned his attention to her. "My mama taught me to be a gentleman, and being a gentleman never goes out of style. You know she'd hit me upside my head if I even thought about letting you cover the bill."

A ghost of a smile appeared on her face. She must have thought about the same thing. Mama Katherine had been half his size, but she never let him intimidate her. She never let anyone intimidate her, for that matter. A thin rail of a woman, she had a tongue sharper than a razor's edge and would get up in his face to give him a piece of her mind if she thought he was getting out of line. She hadn't been able to have kids of her own, but her house had been filled with children for decades. She didn't just take in foster kids—she sought out the most troubled ones, the older kids, the ones nobody else wanted and showered them with love and copious amounts of discipline should they need it.

Almost as quickly as the smile appeared on Ivy's face, it disappeared. "What did you want to talk to me about?"

"I want Katie to know I'm her father."

"No." The answer came swift and hard.

"What do you mean, no?" He sat up. He hadn't known what to expect, but her answer surprised him.

"You don't want to do this."

"I know what I want. I don't need you to explain it to me."

"Why the change?" she asked.

"Because she's my flesh and blood, that's why. Because it's the right thing to do." Did he really need to explain this to her?

The waiter arrived with Ivy's wine and his vodka. She lifted the glass to her lips and gulped down half of it.

She set the glass on the table with a measured motion. "And then what? When you get tired of the role—which we both know you will—you get to disappear? I don't think so. You live in Atlanta, we live here. It's not as if we'd run into each other."

"I'm not going to beg you to recognize my parental rights."

"There's no proof she's your daughter."

Lucas sat back. "That's your story now? We both know she is. You wouldn't have told me she was if she wasn't, so cut the bullshit." He took a sip of his vodka and watched her over the rim of the tumbler. "I can play hard ball, Ivy, if that's what you prefer. It seems first you kidnapped my sperm and now you want to hold my daughter hostage."

Her eyes widened. "I did not kidnap your sperm!" she said in a fierce whisper.

As far as he was concerned, there was no other way to describe what she'd done. "What would you call it?"

"You handed it over."

"Not willingly. The condom broke and you took what didn't belong to you."

"You're being ridiculous."

She took a swallow of wine and pressed a hand to her forehead. He watched her dispassionately, insanely pleased she was beginning to unravel a little bit. At least he wasn't the only one who felt out of sorts.

"Lucas, we both know this isn't something you want. You've made it very clear that you never want to be married and you don't want kids. It's even in your book."

"You read my book?"

"Cover to cover. Very enlightening."

Her confession surprised him. "Did you read the part about a man's rights? A father's rights?"

"Yes, and according to your book, a man has a right to know. Well, you do now, and there's nothing else for you to do." She had it all figured out.

"Oh, there's plenty for me to do. For instance," he leaned forward, one hand on his knee holding the glass of liquor, "I could go to the press and spill the beans about this whole cover up. How the heiress to the Johnson fortune hid the illegitimate birth of her daughter from the biological father and allowed another man to raise his daughter without his knowledge. And how even now she denies him access to his child."

Her family shunned publicity and guarded their privacy with incomparable ferocity. What would she do to prevent a scandal?

Ivy stilled and heat flooded her body, but she immediately rejected his threat. "You wouldn't."

"Try me." Unyielding hardness filled his face.

She sipped her wine. She would need another glass soon. "I'm not proud of what I did, but I don't regret my decision."

"I didn't think you would. I imagine it's not the Johnson way to have regrets." He waited. "What will it be?" Now he was the one pushing her for an answer.

Her gaze swept the interior of the lounge as she weighed her answer. "You can see her, but you can't tell her who you are yet."

"Not gonna happen. We're telling her."

Her gaze fell back on him. "I don't know your intentions."

"My intentions are to get to know my daughter."

"One minute you don't want a child, and the next you do? I'm supposed to believe you're all in?"

"I changed my mind. It's a man's prerogative. Just like it was your prerogative not to take that pill."

His words stung.

No matter what he thought, the choice she made hadn't been an easy one. She'd planned to take it. Had gone so far as to stop at the pharmacy and bought one of the more popular brands, bearing the looks from the attendant at the cash register, picking up a few extra items—a magazine, deodorant, candy—as if somehow they would make the package invisible.

She'd opened the box in her bedroom, but at the last minute didn't go through with it. She could prevent the pregnancy or...what if she didn't? What if she simply allowed nature to take its course? She'd made her decision right then that she wouldn't do it. No matter the circumstances, she would handle the fallout of a baby. If her parents wanted to send her away for a while, she would go. She had considered leaving for their property in Nice, or the beach house in Hawaii, but neither trip had been necessary because Winston had proposed.

Now Lucas was boxing her into a corner. First he hadn't wanted this child, now he did, and he had the audacity to threaten her with a scandal.

"Fine, Lucas, I'll do what you want, but I don't like it."

He smiled, but it was more of a sneer. "Of course. Protect the family name at all costs."

He seemed so angry she doubted the rancor directed at her was solely due to keeping Katie a secret. Was there something else? "What happened to you?" she asked.

His eyes bored into her. "You happened to me. You and your lies about love and your goddamn deceit."

His accusation flew out of left field. "I never lied to you about my feelings. I cared about you very much, once, but you left, remember? So what the hell difference does it make?" Again she had the distinct impression that he wasn't telling her everything.

"You loved me so much you didn't think twice about marrying another man less than two months after we broke up? A man who, according to the article I read, you were secretly engaged to. High school sweethearts."

"You saw that?" He would have been in Asia at the time. Her marriage had been a mere blip in the society pages, only newsworthy because of the blending of two powerful families—the Johnsons with their wealth and the Somersets, part of a political dynasty. Certainly nothing that would make international news.

"Yeah, I saw that," Lucas said. He banged the empty tumbler on the table between them. "Are we going to play by my rules now, or do I start shouting from the mountain top? We both know you can deliver a good scandal."

Her face burned with remembered shame. "You've turned into a cold-hearted bastard. You didn't have to go there." His reference to her youthful indiscretion cut deep. A poor decision had gone terribly awry. She'd shared the story with Lucas in an intimate moment alone, and she resented him bringing it up now. "You win," she said.

"Damn straight."

"But you have to be sure. I've spent my entire life protecting her and giving her as normal a life as possible. She didn't ask to be born into this family, and I've done everything I can to shield her." There were no photos of Katie in circulation, and except for when she was born her name had never been mentioned in articles about the family or the business. "Being a parent takes time and care, and it's not an easy job. You said you didn't want children, and I took you at your word. If you come into her life, you don't get to change your mind."

"What are you trying to say?"

"You better make sure you want this, because if you hurt my baby, you'll live to regret it."

His brows drew together. "Are you threatening me?"

Ivy leaned forward. "You know those billions you said I could have used to find you? If you hurt my daughter, if I have to, I will use every last one of them to make your life a living hell."

CHAPTER NINE

Seconds ticked by as their gazes fused together.

"And you think *I've* changed?" Lucas said with a raised brow. He looked somewhat amused at her threat, almost as if he relished her outburst.

His reaction infuriated her. "We won't have any problems as long as we both know where we stand."

A sardonic smile lifted the corners of his mouth. "Message received loud and clear."

"Good." She ignored how even such a small movement of his lips made her pulse trip and finished her wine. "I'm ready to go."

They stood and the waiter rushed over. Lucas paid for the drinks and Ivy slipped ahead of him, but from the corner of her eye she caught his hand lifting, as if he was about to place it to her lower back again. Tensed, she swung around, but he'd stopped himself.

"Old habits die hard," he explained in his lazy drawl, "but don't worry, I haven't forgotten you don't want me to touch you." A muscle in his jaw flexed.

Without a word Ivy turned back around and marched ahead of him, wishing she could outrun the torrent of emotions that gripped her. It was hard as hell to maintain a frosty outward appearance when her entire body burned with the heat of a furnace. She had to stop imagining him doing things to her, such as dragging his tongue up the length of her back, or gently biting her neck, or—heaven help her—sucking on her collarbone.

They entered the elevator in silence, he in one corner, she in the other. Between them an older couple who'd come in behind them spoke quietly to each other. On the fifth floor the couple exited and left her and Lucas alone.

"Makes me wonder, though," Lucas said in a conversational tone.

Ivy flicked her gaze to him. He looked mighty smug over there, with his hands stuffed into his pockets, watching her. "What are you talking about?"

He walked over and stopped mere inches away. Her stomach clenched, her reaction to him impulsive and ingrained on a cellular level.

Lucas rested his shoulder against the wall and looked down at her, one of the few men who could when she wore heels. "I can't help but wonder why you don't want me to touch you." His gaze traced her shape, a bold perusal that made her skin prickle.

"There's no why, I simply don't. Is it really so hard for you to believe?" She averted her eyes to the numbers lighting up as they ascended the hotel tower. She prayed for a faster climb so she could escape the confining cabin. "I'm sorry I'm not falling all over you like I did nine years ago. It must be terribly disappointing."

He dipped his head to her ear, and every muscle fiber tightened at his nearness. His scent filled the air around her, a woodsy fragrance with base notes of sandalwood. She clenched her purse as she fought the temptation to brush her cheek against his to test the texture of his beard. If she moved her head even a fraction to the right, they'd touch.

"What's disappointing," he said softly, "is seeing you do such a poor acting job."

Ivy stared straight ahead. "I didn't think it was possible for you to get any more arrogant than you were before, but you've exceeded my expectations."

He laughed, his breath a whisper against the shell of her ear, sending tiny tremors racing down her spine. "It's not arrogance, Ivy. I happen to be able to read body language, and darlin', based on yours, I'd say you're as nervous as a long-tailed cat in a room full of rocking chairs." He flashed his teeth at her, and she desperately wanted to slap the grin off his face.

She was still debating whether or not to do it when the doors opened. "We're here," she said pointedly.

He stepped back and allowed her to lead the way to her condo.

Inside, on her own turf, her confidence bolstered, and when her daughter rushed to her from the table where she and Janelle had been working on a crossword puzzle, her mouth lifted into a smile.

Katie peered up at Lucas. "Hi. You're the writer."

"That's right," he said.

Ivy dismissed Janelle, and after catching up with her daughter about her day, she steered Katie into the living room and they sat on the sofa beside each other.

Lucas sat catty-cornered from them in an overstuffed chair, and he ran his palms down his pants. They'd grown sweaty watching his daughter and Ivy interact.

Katie pushed her glasses up on her nose and looked from one to the other. "Am I in trouble?" she asked.

"No," Ivy said. "You're not in any trouble, but I—we—have something to tell you."

His daughter's expression changed as he and Ivy explained that he was her father. She looked confused, and rightly so. It was hard for him to comprehend he had a child, and clearly hard for her to understand how she could have another father. For her entire life she'd believed one man to be her father, and now she was told a complete stranger was. The guy she'd met in the building where her mother worked.

"Your first dad took care of you while Lucas was away. Now he's back, and he can be your father the same way Winston was."

"So I have two dads?" Katie asked.

"Something like that," Lucas interjected. "But I'm your real dad." He wanted to make that clear.

"Oh." She still appeared confused, and she looked at her mother, seeking guidance.

Ivy placed a hand on her daughter's slender shoulders. "He wants to get to know you and spend time with you," she explained. "Would that be okay?"

Katie's lower lip quivered and her shoulders curled forward. With a vehement shake of her head, she said, "No. My daddy's dead and I don't want another daddy!"

"Katie!"

The little girl—his daughter—raced off down the hall toward the bedrooms. With an apologetic look in his direction, Ivy hurried after her.

Lucas sat there, dumbfounded. He was still getting used to the idea of being her father, but deep down he'd hoped she'd be excited and maybe fling her arms around him. Because that's what he'd wanted to do—sweep her up in his arms in a big hug and start bonding right away.

When she re-entered the room, Ivy appeared embarrassed. She had the same apologetic expression on her face as before and waved her hand vaguely, struggling to find the right words.

Lucas didn't give her a chance to speak. "She doesn't want to come back," he said.

She shook her head, pity in her eyes, and he hated it. "We should take it slow. This is new for all of us."

He nodded his understanding and rose from the chair. Ivy escorted him to the front door.

"Give her time," she said quietly. "She'll warm up to you once she gets to know you better."

Lucas had his doubts, but this setback wouldn't stop him from being a part of Katie's life. "I'm not giving up," he said. "I'll be back tomorrow. And the next day. And the day after that."

Having Katie accept him as her father would become his focus. It hadn't occurred to him she wouldn't want him in her life, and he hadn't expected rejection could cut so deeply.

CHAPTER TEN

At the desk in his hotel room, Lucas stared at the computer screen. His advice column was due to *Essence* in a couple of days, but he wasn't in the mood to answer questions.

Dear Lucas,

My boyfriend and I have been living together for three years. He's perfect in every way, but whenever I mention marriage, he clams up. I don't understand it. We get along well and we share everything. We live together, for goodness' sake! He says we don't need a piece of paper and why fix what isn't broken. I think I can change his mind, but my best friend thinks I'm a fool and I'm wasting my time with him. I believe love is worth fighting for. What do you think?

Confused in Virginia

Lucas tapped out his response.

Dear Confused,

Your friend is right.

His editor would never let him get away with such a cryptic answer, but it was the best he could do right now. His mind was too bogged down with thoughts of Ivy and Katie.

Flickers of light from the television bounced off the walls. He glanced at it to see a local reporter giving the nightly news, but he had the volume turned down too low to hear.

How would things have been different if he hadn't left after their summer fling? He wouldn't admit it to Ivy, but he'd had doubts about leaving.

Lucas felt the warmth of her naked body as she lay on top of him.

"Wake up, sleepyhead," Ivy said softly. She kissed his neck, shoulders, and the middle of his back.

He groaned. "I'm tired. You wore me out."

She giggled. "You promised to take me to breakfast before you go to work."

"Did I?"

"Yes. You're not reneging, are you?" Her tongue traced his shoulder bone. They weren't going anywhere if she kept that up.

He turned and flipped her onto her back. Her eyes shined like little brown jewels, and moments like this made him want to forget the teaching contract in Korea so he wouldn't have to leave her.

"How hungry are you?" he asked. Maybe they could have a quickie before they left for breakfast.

"I'm so hungry my belly thinks my throat's been cut."

He busted out laughing. "I'm going to stop teaching you all these Southern expressions. The words are right but the accent sucks."

"It does not! I nailed the accent."

"Yes, it does suck. You think you're doing such a good job, don't you? Bless your heart."

"Don't you bless my heart." She hit him in the shoulder and he pinned her arms above her head.

He nuzzled her throat and then sucked the sensitive spot where her neck and shoulder met. "What do you want me to do then? This okay?"

"Maybe," she said, pretending to be upset by pouting.

"How about this?" He licked her nipple and sucked the tip into his mouth.

Ivy moaned. "You know, I'm not that hungry after all."

"You're not? You sure?" He licked the tight peak of her other breast and she arched higher into his mouth.

She gasped. "Yes, I'm sure."

She wriggled beneath him, spreading her legs to open her body for him and lifting her hips to grind her mound against his erection.

"Hold on, let me get a condom."

"Hurry."

When he was sheathed in latex, he slid into her, slow and easy. She gasped and thrust up against him. Watching her lose it was almost as exciting as getting off himself.

She was so sexy, driving him crazy with how much she loved sex. Her desire for it matched his. It was limitless, all-consuming. Her response to his touch was always frenzied and passionate. Not the fake stuff some women did, like they were actresses in a porn flick where they said everything just right and had to move just right so they didn't muss their hair. No, with Ivy he could tell she really loved it and lost herself in the sensations.

"Lucas…" She gripped his shoulders.

"I'm right here." Her feminine walls contracted around him and her fingernails dug into his skin. She came hard, her breathless cries filling the small bedroom. Her face wrenched into a grimace of pleasure, and his brain took a snapshot of that expression like he'd done many times before. He strived to put that pained look on her face. As if his lovemaking was so exceptional it surpassed her expectations and filled her with the exquisiteness of an orgasm so sweet it pained her.

"I'm not going anywhere," he said.

Lucas groaned and rubbed his aching groin. He knew from experience the bulge in his pants wouldn't go away any time soon.

His cell phone, resting on the table in front of the television, started ringing. The unique tone was earmarked for Priscilla Graw, an aspiring model/actress/dancer or producer/director/entrepreneur, depending on the day and mood. Priscilla dipped her toes into more creative pursuits than anyone else he knew. To date, none of her ventures had proved successful.

He and she had been dating off and on over the past five years. Currently they were off, and he hadn't spoken to her in a few months.

"Hey," he said.

"Did I wake you?" she asked. She sounded like she was in bed herself. Her voice carried the warmth of slumber, as if she'd been sleeping only moments before. He imagined her pushing her thick corkscrew curls off her forehead.

"No, I'm wide awake and working on a column."

"We haven't talked in a long time. How'd everything go?"

She was asking about the tour, but his mind veered to the conversation with Katie and the negative outcome.

He sat down and dropped his head on the back of the sofa. "The tour went well. I sold a lot of books at each stop, and I'm in Seattle now. I spoke in a packed auditorium at an event a few days ago."

"I'm happy for you, baby. Maybe you'll be able to hit one of those bestsellers lists soon."

"Maybe. That would be nice." He held no illusions about that type of success. He was happy for what success he already had.

"You don't sound pleased."

"I am." But the conversation with Katie still dogged him, dousing any excitement he had felt about his trip up until this point.

"When will you be back in Atlanta?"

"I have some things to take care of out here. I won't be back for a bit."

"Oh?" She never came right out and questioned him, and he didn't know if her reluctance was the result of trust or simply that she didn't want to rock the boat of their off and on relationship.

"I saw an old girlfriend, and…it turns out I have a daughter."

"*Oh.*"

The quiet on the other end of the line prompted him to sit up and continue. "I want to spend a little time getting to know her better. Katie's her name. I was with her and her mother tonight, but it was mainly about Katie—not her mother." Why he felt the need to mention that he had no idea.

"I didn't think you'd want to spend time with your ex," Priscilla said in an overly neutral voice. She always tiptoed around him and his feelings, as if she was afraid of upsetting him. "So she just kept your child a secret from you?"

"Yeah. We ran into each other and I found out by accident."

"How old's your kid?" Priscilla asked.

"Eight."

"That's a long time."

"Yeah." Lucas filled her in on the details.

"Wait a minute." The slumberous quality disappeared from Priscilla's voice and he heard the bed linens rustle as she changed positions. "Are you kidding me? Your child's mother is a Johnson—a member of the family who owns Full Moon beer and the restaurant chains The Brew Pub and Ivy's?"

"You know the family?" He had to admit he was surprised.

"I don't *know* them, but I know of them. They don't make the news often—mostly it's the oldest son…oh, what's his name…Cyrus. I saw him on the cover of a magazine once. I stopped to read it because, well, it's not too often you read about black billionaires. They mentioned how he's practically been running the company since his twenties, after his father died suddenly. A drunk driver killed him or something. They had a three-year decline in sales recently, but he turned it around with a new marketing campaign. They're one of the richest families in the country."

Lucas was surprised Priscilla had paid that much attention to the family.

"You're a lucky man," she continued.

"Why am I lucky?"

"Because they're super rich."

He snorted and walked to the window. He drew apart the drapes and looked out at the urban landscape. "Their money doesn't mean anything to me."

"Are you sure? If you worked your way back into your baby mama's good graces, you'd be set."

He cringed. He couldn't tell if she was kidding or not. Plus he hated the phrase 'baby mama.' "No way am I interested in sinking my claws into the family fortune. I just want to get to know my kid." He still didn't know how he would fit into the picture, especially since Katie had made it clear she didn't want him around.

"You should consider yourself lucky. You don't have to worry about child support. I told you how much my brother pays to his ex-wife. He stays broke." She sighed. They'd had plenty of conversations about the unfairness of her brother's payments mandated in the divorce decree. "So when will I see you again?"

She must want something. Every time they'd broken up over the past five years, Priscilla had been the one to leave him. She would grow tired of his behavior, his lack of interest—his whatever she chose to fling at him in a fit of anger when she stormed out. But she always came back.

Usually she'd call and need his help with something inconsequential. She'd ask if he could review a car repair estimate and give his opinion on whether or not it was reasonable. Or could he come over and help her move a piece of furniture. She obviously used these tasks as an excuse to reach out to him again.

"I'm not sure when I'll be back. Not for a couple of weeks. I don't have any classes at Mercer until the spring, and I can work around most of my promotional gigs until it's time to start traveling again."

"I was hoping you'd be back sooner," she said, her voice filled with disappointment. Yeah, she wanted something.

"How are you doing? You need anything?"

"Well, now that you mention it…I'm a little short on rent this month. Could you loan me a couple hundred dollars?"

To be considered a loan, the assumption was that the money would be repaid, but she never repaid him when money was exchanged between them.

"I'll transfer the money into your account tonight," he said.

"Thank you, baby." Her voice lowered. "I'll take good care of you when you get back."

He chuckled. "I know you will. I'll call you when I'm back in the ATL."

Lucas disconnected the call and continued to stare out the window. He had to figure out how to win Katie over, and he didn't have a clue how to do it.

CHAPTER ELEVEN

"Have a good day," Ivy called as her daughter scrambled from the car. Katie raced toward the front of the school building, meeting up with one of her friends halfway there.

At first glance, the wooded grounds of St. Francis's Academy looked more like that of a small college campus. Most of the children who attended came from wealthy families. In the afternoons, the grounds resembled the parking lot of a high-end car dealership as parents or drivers arrived in Mercedes, Maybachs, and other luxury vehicles to pick up the children.

Ivy settled into the soft leather of the black Cadillac, a vehicle custom-designed to accommodate her needs. The front and back seats could be separated by privacy glass and the body was constructed of reinforced steel.

Lloyd pulled out of the parking lot. "You okay, ma'am?" he asked.

He must have noted the difference in her this morning, the noncommittal answers she'd given to Katie as her daughter chatted up a storm, excited about the first day back at school.

"They grow up so fast," she said, her gaze meeting his in the mirror.

She'd been thinking about her daughter, but she'd also thought about Lucas. There had been no improvement in the relationship between Lucas and Katie over the past few days, but Lucas continued to show up despite Katie's profound lack of interest in him. She felt bad for him. Katie's cool reception was all her fault.

"Nothing you can do about them growing up," Lloyd said. "It

happens. It seems only yesterday my kids were her age." A strand of nostalgia filled his voice.

Lloyd seldom gave details about his personal life. Whenever he did, he focused on his children. In his mid-forties and divorced, he had one adult child married and two in college. He had a military background and doubled as her bodyguard. He'd been hired from a private security firm not long after Ivy's mother had learned of a wealthy acquaintance's daughter being kidnapped when their car was boxed in. Under the traditional black chauffeur cap and black suit was a buzz cut and a large, muscular man. Though he remained mostly quiet, they had developed a comfortable rapport over the years.

When Lloyd dropped her off, Ivy made a quick stop at her office and then headed to Cyrus's office. This morning she had a meeting with him and Trenton in the small room off Cyrus's office. When she entered, she found her brothers already waiting for her with the scent of fresh-brewed coffee filling the air.

Cyrus sat at the head of the small conference table. Dressed in a dark suit, lavender shirt, and purple and black striped tie, he looked like the man in charge that he was. Trenton, on the other hand, had his chair tipped back and only wore a shirt and tie, minus the suit jacket. He was the youngest in the family and anyone who didn't know their family history would stare because of his lighter skin and green eyes. He clearly didn't match.

It amused Ivy to see the wheels turning as people silently questioned his background. The more daring ones, who outright asked if he had a different parent, received an honest answer. Trenton was their cousin, but he'd been raised with them from a young age after his parents passed away. Despite not having the same parents, he was as much her brother as the ones she shared parents with.

Cyrus had suggested having these occasional meetings, where they could meet and discuss business and brainstorm privately without staff present. The three of them were the most active members of the family in the business.

Sometimes their mother would conference in, and if they could catch Xavier, their brother who was in Africa at the moment, he would participate. Her twin, Gavin, never took part in their business meetings. He never participated in anything, which filled her with sadness. They used to be so close, but he mostly stayed away now, collecting his monthly allowance and living his own life apart from them. She had no idea where he was at the moment, but when he was ready he'd call and let them know that he was still alive.

"Don't tell me I'm late," Ivy said, pouring herself a cup of coffee.

"Right on time," Trenton replied. "I was trying to squeeze some additional funds out of the head honcho so I could work my magic for the Great American Beer Festival and Oktoberfest." He grinned mischievously. Trenton oversaw sales and marketing and special events such as the anniversary celebration still underway.

"And I told our dear brother that he would have to work with the same budget he did last year," Cyrus said.

Ivy took a seat. Her brothers always managed to be at odds with each other about one thing or another, but it was good-natured ribbing brought about by their different personalities.

They spent about fifteen minutes discussing the direction of the company. Cyrus gave them an update on a possible trademark infringement with a brewery out of New Jersey that was causing confusion with their customers and then swiveled his chair in Ivy's direction. "What's going on with you?"

"Nothing much. Katie's father is here." She hadn't meant to blurt out the news in that way, but there was no better time than the present. There weren't very many people she could share this with. Not yet, anyway.

Both her brothers sat up straight.

"I was talking about the restaurant group," Cyrus said.

"Her biological—her real father?" Trenton asked.

"The only one. He wants a relationship with her." Her gaze bounced between them.

"What rock did he crawl out from under, and what else does he want?" Cyrus, always the cynic, asked.

"Nothing."

"Everybody wants something, Ivy."

"Not him. He doesn't want money," she assured him.

"Not yet."

"Not ever. He never cared about my money."

Most people who learned her true identity fell into two camps. One set grew excited because they saw knowing her as an opportunity to get inside the upper echelons of society, or worse, expected her to shower them with money, gifts, or "loans" for business ideas. The other group steered clear of her, either out of a sense of inadequacy or the assumption that she lived her life in excess. Her money simply made them uncomfortable. Lucas had displayed neither behavior.

"What does he want, then?" Cyrus said.

"He wants to get to know his daughter."

Cyrus tapped his finger on the sheets of paper in front of him. "I guess the secret will be out of the bag soon enough. All the maneuvering we did to keep this quiet will be for naught." He voice held an irritated edge to it.

Ivy jerked her head in her brother's direction. "It doesn't have to be a thing, Cyrus."

"It's always a thing," Cyrus snapped. His displeasure was almost tangible. "Then we'll end up having to clean up another mess."

"You can be a real ass, you know that? I will clean up my own mess, thank you very much."

"Damn, Cy, cut her some slack," Trenton said.

"I'm trying to make a point," Cyrus said.

"What exactly is your point?" Ivy crossed her arms over her chest and glared at her brother.

"What I'm trying to say," Cyrus said slowly, his anger simmering like hers, "is that we need to be careful. There's more at stake than our family reputation. Winston's father is a well-respected senator, and even though the media doesn't know the truth about Katie's paternity, once they get wind of it, we'll have a mess on our hands."

Josiah Somerset was Ivy's dead husband's father and had already started his campaign for his sophomore term in the Senate.

"I know, Cyrus, I'm not an idiot."

"Well then what's the plan, Ivy?" Cyrus asked.

"He's her father and they should get to know each other. That's the plan." She took a deep breath and splayed her hands on the table. She looked at each of her brothers in turn. "I didn't expect the situation to play out this way, but now that Lucas knows, he and Katie should have a relationship. I can't avoid it, and I shouldn't try."

"How'd he find out?"

"He came by my office unexpectedly. He saw Katie, talked to her, and he put two and two together. He was the guy you noticed at the anniversary party."

"You should have told me who he was when I asked you at the party," Cyrus said.

"What would you have done? Had him killed?" Ivy held up her hand. "Don't answer that." She wouldn't put anything past her brother and his need to protect the family.

"What do you plan to do about Winston's family?" Cyrus asked.

Ivy shrugged. "I'll have to tell them he's in her life now, but that won't change anything for them. They've known almost from the beginning that she wasn't their granddaughter and didn't care." Having Winston's parents accept Katie as part of the family had made the deception easier.

"Mother will want to meet him," Trenton said.

"I don't think now is the best time," Ivy said. "I want to take this slow so Lucas and Katie can get to know each other first. Things have been a bit...bumpy."

"You'll have to introduce him to other people, too."

"To be honest, outside of the family, I doubt anyone will care." At least that's what she told herself. She'd done a good job of staying out of the news for years. There was no reason that should change.

Cyrus spoke again. "If you need—"

"Cyrus, let me handle this." She had to cut him off before he tried to take over. "The last thing I need is for you to start meddling."

"I don't meddle."

Ivy raised a skeptical brow and Trenton fake coughed.

Cyrus pursed his lips. "Fine, but would you do me a favor? Be careful with this guy. You knew him when you were much younger, but for all we know, he could have an agenda now. When he has time to think about the situation, he could become greedy. Equally important is how you handle this. I remember how torn up you were after your relationship with him ended. Do you still have feelings for him?"

"No." She answered too quickly, and her older brother's eyes narrowed perceptively. She rushed on. "As you pointed out, I was younger then. I'm going to continue dating, like I've been doing, and nothing will change for him, either. He's living the bachelor lifestyle, flying from city to city and seeing multiple women. There's no chance of us rekindling any kind of relationship."

"You sure about that?" That was Trenton. Even he doubted her. "You have a child together."

"Of course I'm sure." Her voice hardened, her resolve firmed. "Years have passed since we were together, and lots of people have children together and move on from each other. Why would Lucas and I be any different?"

CHAPTER TWELVE

Trying to win over his daughter was turning out to be a lot more difficult than Lucas had expected. However, her reluctance to see him and lack of interest in spending time with him didn't quench the desire he had to see her and connect. Her apathy only made him want it more.

Whenever he saw her, he experienced so many emotions. Wonder, at this little person who carried his blood in her veins. Disbelief, that he'd been kept in the dark for so long. And a deep affection that overwhelmed him as he examined her face and heard her voice, knowing she derived half her genetic makeup from him.

Resentment, an uglier emotion, also infiltrated his thoughts. Another man, an imposter, had filled the position of father for years and quite well, apparently. So well, Katie didn't want anyone else in his place. While Lucas had been cheated out of all the important milestones in his daughter's life, Winston had experienced them all. Her first words, her first steps, and her first day of school.

After several visits trying to win over Katie, Lucas was at a loss. She hadn't warmed up to him anymore than before. She treated him like a stranger and sat quietly while he talked about his life in Atlanta and what he did for a living. When he asked her about school and her family, her monosyllabic answers made it clear she'd rather be anywhere else doing anything else but sitting with him.

Finally, though, he had an idea, one he hoped would break the ice between them.

****

Ivy opened the door, surprised to see Lucas standing on the other side. "You're early," she said.

Her trainer had left a few minutes ago after an intensive yoga session, and her skin was still damp with sweat. She hadn't had a chance to shower and change and wore the yoga pants and fitted tank from her class. She felt grimy, sweaty, and decidedly unattractive.

"I hope you don't mind," Lucas said.

Strangely, he seemed excited. His interactions with Katie over the past few days had been awkward, to say the least, but he appeared renewed. Her heart had gone out to him as he arrived night after night, only to be greeted by Katie's tepid responses. He held a rectangular package in his hand, giftwrapped with a pretty white bow on it. Her heart hurt a little bit more for him. He'd resorted to bribery for his daughter's affection.

"No, of course I don't mind. Come in." She opened the door wider and let him in.

His muscular physique filled the small entryway. He was dressed business casual in a pair of dark slacks and a maroon shirt with the sleeves rolled up almost to his elbows, revealing hair sprinkled along his sinewy forearms. The undone top button on his shirt offered a peek at more hair on his chest.

Could he be any more sexy? Any more virile?

The first time she'd seen him years ago, she'd assumed he must be an athlete because of his size, but nothing could have been farther from the truth. Except recreationally, Lucas hadn't played sports. He hadn't fit her idea of the passionate writer and bibliophile, but as she'd gotten to know him, she'd seen that side of him. More than anything, she loved listening to him do spoken word. It always turned her on to hear him recite his poems on stage in his deep, sexy voice.

"Katie finished her homework with the babysitter, and she's at the dining room table writing."

"You just came in from exercising, I see," Lucas said as they walked back.

His conversational tone held a warm undercurrent that made her self-aware. If she turned around she knew she'd see him watching her body. And of course there was plenty for him to see in the clinging pants and body-hugging top.

"I get in a few hours a week," she replied. She could practically feel his gaze on her—and the tiny hairs on her skin rose as a shiver quivered under her skin.

She brought him into the open room. "Katie, your father's here."

Katie looked up from the book she'd been writing in. She'd had a long talk with her daughter the night before about being more polite when her father came around. When she muttered a dispirited, "Hi," and dragged from the table, it was obvious the talk hadn't worked.

Lucas lowered to his haunches in front of his daughter. Ivy stepped back to give them a modicum of privacy, but she remained close enough so she could satisfy her curiosity about what was in the prettily wrapped package.

"I brought you something," he said. He handed Katie the gift.

"What is it?" she asked.

"Open it and see."

Katie looked over at her and Ivy smiled encouragingly. She opened the package slowly, taking her time to remove the paper as if she expected something to jump out at her. Finally, she revealed a purple, leather bound journal. A warm glow lit in Ivy's chest. He'd remembered purple was Katie's favorite color.

Katie turned the book over in her hands. "What is it?"

"It's called a journal," Lucas explained. "I remembered you said you liked to write down your thoughts. If you're going to do it, you need to do it the right way, the same as a writer would. I mean, you're a writer, right?"

Katie nodded vigorously.

"I thought that's what you said." He unhooked the latch and opened it for her to see the lined pages. A purple pen lay attached to a wide band of elastic on the inside. "Every good writer needs a journal to write her thoughts, dreams, and ideas. So, you write down your thoughts in here, and then you lock it up so no one gets to read it. It'll be your own private diary of whatever you're thinking or feeling. For your eyes only." He produced a key for the lock hanging off the zipper's pull tab and Katie took it.

She hugged the gift to her chest and rewarded Lucas with a small smile. "Thank you."

Lucas stood and Katie looked up at him, then at her mother. "Can I go write in my journal?"

"Well..." Ivy said. Lucas had come over to spend time with her, and now she was running off.

"It's okay. That's what it's for," he said. He seemed satisfied with the results of his actions.

Katie hurried off down the hall and left them alone together, and Lucas immediately blew a burst of air from his mouth. He must have been more nervous than he let on. After Katie's constant rejection, it must be a relief to finally get a positive reaction.

"That went well," Ivy said.

"Better than I thought," he agreed with a grin.

A genuine, full-on grin lit up his eyes and made her heart do a treacherous somersault. He had always smiled like that—a dazzling expression—as if his entire being were involved in the act. The perpetual smile around his eyes had been one of the things that had made him attractive to her. He had a *joie de vivre* that she hadn't mastered at the time, clearly loving every second of life. Coupled with his unique blend of beauty and masculinity, he'd been downright irresistible.

"When in doubt, getting a woman a gift is always a good way to soften her up," Ivy quipped.

He chuckled. "I know a lot about women, but I didn't think little girls were exactly the same. I should have known."

Ivy clasped her hands in front of her. "Um…would you like to stay for dinner?"

He shook his head. "I'll have to take a rain check. I've got a writing deadline to meet, but I wanted to see her tonight."

"I appreciate you doing all of this."

He frowned. "All of what?"

"Spending time with her and hanging in there even though she hasn't exactly been welcoming."

He shrugged his broad shoulders. "It's been what, a week? It's understandable. Like you said, it'll take time for her to get used to me. Oh, before I forget." He pulled something out of his pocket. "Here's the second key to the journal, in case she loses hers or you need to do any snooping."

Ivy took it, careful not to touch him. "Look at you, already thinking like a parent."

They smiled at each other, and her chest tightened a little. Seconds ticked by and she shifted from one foot to the next.

"So where do you go to work out?" Lucas asked.

"I've been doing more yoga lately, and I do it here. The trainer comes by and works with me for an hour. I go down to the hotel gym and get on the machines when I want to really sweat." The last part sounded like sexual innuendo and her cheeks heated.

He raised an eyebrow and observed her from head to toe. "Don't tell me you're trying to lose weight?"

She blushed at the shock in his voice. "You know how we women are. We always think we can stand to lose a few pounds."

In all honesty a few years ago she'd given up trying to lose any more weight and accepted her figure. So her stomach was softer and not as flat and firm as it had been in her early twenties. Her main goal was to stay healthy, and stressing about losing an extra ten pounds that she'd then have to be vigilant about keeping off was not on her list of priorities.

Both of Lucas's brows raised in surprise this time. "And you feel that way? Like you could stand to lose a few pounds?"

"Maybe a pound here or there." She lifted one shoulder, suggesting it didn't really matter, but she wondered what he thought. She wasn't the same lithe young woman he'd met nine years ago.

"Well, whatever you do..." His gaze raked boldly over her and lingered, settling on the arc of her hips and thighs. She couldn't read his eyes because he'd lowered his lids and those thick, pretty lashes of his shielded his thoughts. "Lose all the weight you want. Just don't lose that ass."

She stopped breathing. What was she supposed to say to such a comment?

She ran her hands down her hips to get rid of their dampness, but the action ended up drawing attention to her figure. Lucas's eyes followed the movement, and heat mushroomed from her pelvis to other parts of her body. She swallowed nervously. Her thoughts veered into dangerous territory, such as wondering what kind of sensation she'd experience if he kissed one of her butt cheeks and she could feel the bristles of his beard rub across her bottom.

Lucas was an ass man, and he'd made no secret of how much he'd enjoyed hers.

"Mmm..." His tongue stroked over the curve of her fleshy bottom. He pinched the soft skin between his teeth. She gasped, moving restlessly, lifting her hips higher. Moisture pooled in the apex of her thighs.

He cupped both cheeks in his big hands and squeezed. He kissed each one in turn.

"You done turned me into an ass kisser."

As if he guessed her thoughts, one corner of his mouth lifted into a smile. "I'll be more considerate of your time tomorrow," he said. He didn't move; he just stood there.

"Thanks." She couldn't think of another single thing to say. The complication of a sentence was too much for her brain to handle at the moment.

The silence between them lengthened and as he watched her, she shifted to the other foot and cleared her throat. "So…um…"

"Guess I better head out," he said. Finally, he turned and walked to the front door.

Still shaken, Ivy stumbled along behind him. "Coming by early wasn't a problem," she said. "You're welcome any time. It's good for you and Katie to spend as much time together as possible so you can bond before you leave to go back to Atlanta."

"Agreed." He paused outside the open door. "I'll give you a call tomorrow if I plan to come by earlier."

"Sounds good."

His eyes ran down her body one more time, as if imprinting the image in his mind. Her fingers tightened on the doorknob as she fought the flush of heat that covered her skin.

"Good night, princess," he said softly.

She opened her mouth to remind him not to call her that and stopped. Knowing Lucas, he hadn't forgotten. The pet name didn't annoy her, it was just too intimate, reminding her of what they'd shared in the past.

Ivy stuck her head out the door to watch him walk down the hallway, as sexy as ever and moving with panther-like grace. He had a wide, bow-legged stride like he was hung between the legs. Which, she knew, he was.

She slammed the door shut and rested her head against it. "Breathe."

She should be over him. Sure, there had been times when she'd thought about him and reminisced about their months together. It was only natural when each day she stared into a pair of eyes heart-achingly similar to his.

She placed a hand over her rapidly beating heart.

The last thing she needed was to develop feelings for Lucas again. She couldn't let the wall of civility erected between them crumble under the weight of something as simple as attraction. He couldn't give her what she wanted. She knew that from first-hand experience.

CHAPTER THIRTEEN

It was nachos night, and Lucas had received strict instructions to bring his appetite. Once a month Katie could have whatever meal she chose, and this month she'd chosen nachos. Ivy had called to let him know Katie had invited him to dinner, and how could he possibly refuse the invitation?

He followed Ivy back to the spacious kitchen, from which they had a view of the living room. It contained top grade appliances—a Sub-Zero refrigerator and wine cooler, Miele dishwasher, microwave, and gas stove. It was also large enough to comfortably accommodate several people working there at the same time.

"Anything I can do to help?" he asked.

A pan of ground beef and beans simmered on one of the burners, and he smelled the distinctive aroma of cumin and onions. Ivy looked up from the cutting board where she was back to chopping fresh cilantro for the pico de gallo. "You can get the glasses and beer. I thought we'd try a new winter brew one of our brewmasters blended, if you're interested?"

"Sounds good to me," Lucas said. "I'll be your beer guinea pig."

"No beer for me, thank you," Katie piped up. She burst into giggles.

"That's right." Ivy bumped hips with her daughter and joined in the laugh. "There's juice in the fridge for the little one."

Watching them, Lucas couldn't help but smile. Mother and daughter worked side by side in the kitchen, and although Katie's task was minor in comparison, it was clear having some responsibility in the meal preparation was important to her.

"When did you learn to cook?" he asked Ivy. He grabbed two bottles of Winter Lager and held them up.

"Mommy's a great cook," Katie announced.

Ivy nodded her approval at the beer in his hands. "That's them. They flopped last year, so we're trying a new formula. So far it's tested well in the pubs, but this is the first time I'm trying it out." She sprinkled salt from her fingertips into the pot and gave the meat mixture a stir. "I've learned a lot about cooking in the past eight years or so," she informed him.

They worked in silence for a few minutes, and it felt cozy. Almost like they were a real...family. The thought snuck up on him and he shook off the sentimentality. This was nice and all, but it wasn't what he wanted. This type of tame existence was for other men who didn't crave excitement the way he did. He had a great life in Atlanta, and he liked traveling and meeting different people—especially women. He could still do all that even as he learned to nail down this father-thing. At least he hoped so.

He and Katie made the salad dressing based on Ivy's instructions. Then he poured it on the salad and gave Katie the important task of tossing it. While Ivy placed the food and pico de gallo in serving dishes, he and Katie set the table. Every time he caught his daughter looking at him, he'd wink at her and she'd laugh.

Finally, they sat down to dinner. The nachos were laden down with meat and beans, melted cheese, and over the top they each scattered healthy doses of pico de gallo. He listened to Katie talk about her friends and classes at school. She'd never shared this much information with him, and she sounded excited about her Language Arts class. Pride filled him. He couldn't help but be happy that in some small way she might have taken after him, even though he hadn't been a presence in her life.

"These are great," Lucas said around a bite, during a lull in the conversation.

"Don't talk with your mouth full," Katie chastised him.

"Hey, I'm the adult," he teased back, and tweaked her nose.

He sensed Ivy's eyes on him and met her gaze across the table. She smiled and took a drink of beer.

"What do you think of the brew?" she asked.

"I like it," he answered. She didn't look at him again. He wanted her to, but he pushed away the unwanted ache for some kind of connection and continued eating.

After dinner, Ivy watched Lucas and Katie work on a crossword puzzle, something else they had in common. Katie sat close to her father on the sofa while Ivy used her tablet to prepare the monthly goals for the area managers in the restaurant group.

Every so often her daughter attempted to include her in the activity.

"Mommy, what's a four-letter word for masculine?"

"Mommy, what's a three-letter word for adversary?"

"Mommy, what's a three-letter word for luau garland?"

"Lei," Ivy answered, proud she'd actually known the answer to that one.

As the night wore on, she finished up her project and was about to go clean up the kitchen when Lucas whispered, "She's out."

Katie had nodded off and was leaning against his arm. Seeing the two of them together in that way made such a sweet image, she wanted to take a picture.

"She sure is." That was one thing about her daughter, she fell asleep easily and would soon be deep in slumber. "Come on, munchkin."

Ivy brought her to her feet and she grumbled as she trudged back to the bedroom, leaning on her mother, eyes half-closed. Ivy settled her into bed before heading back out to the living room and found Lucas clearing the table.

"I can do that," she said.

"The least I can do is load the dishwasher since you fed me," he replied with a good-natured smile. His attitude had gone through a complete one-eighty. He certainly was no longer angry at her, but she didn't know what to make of it.

"If you insist," she said to cover the jitters that overcame her. "But the dishwasher's broken and I haven't taken the time to get a repairman in here to look at it yet."

"Then I'll help you wash," Lucas offered.

They stacked dishes on top of one another and took them into the kitchen.

It felt strange to have a man in her home. Particularly one she was attracted to. It would be difficult to explain her relationship with Winston. They'd been more like friends than husband and wife.

Over dinner she'd caught herself watching Lucas, drinking him in. His playfulness with Katie had roused feelings she couldn't ignore. She used to imagine doing things with him, like hanging wallpaper or picking out fabric swatches for furniture together. And now, having him here felt so right. But those thoughts were dangerous. They needed to get along to co-parent. Nothing more.

Ivy ran water in the sink and watched as suds foamed over the dishes. "Maybe being friends isn't such a bad idea," she said. "You know, like you suggested when you came by my office."

"I don't guess we have much of a choice. We have to get along."

She nodded her agreement.

"Want one?" He stuck his hand under her nose with a cinnamon Altoid between his fingers.

"You trying to tell me something?" she asked with a cocked eyebrow.

"All I'm saying is, we both had nachos." A lopsided grin twisted the corner of his mouth. He should stop smiling, because it drew her attention to his mouth each and every time, which made it hard as hell to remain detached.

"Gee, thanks, but my hands are wet. I'll get one in a minute."

He held the candy closer to her face. "Open your mouth."

For tense seconds neither of them moved. Then slowly, she parted her lips and he slipped in the candy. His thumb brushed her lower lip and heat streaked down her chest to the spot between her legs.

Cinnamon flavor burst in her mouth. "Thanks."

"You're welcome." His voice sounded low and raspy, and he stepped back, as if he suddenly realized they were standing too close. He lifted one of the mints into his own mouth and pulled his thumb in between his lips as if—as if he was tasting her.

A startled expression filled his eyes and he stared at his thumb. Then he snapped the tin closed and shoved it into his pants pocket.

Rattled, Ivy turned off the water. The sink was almost filled to the top.

"I'll wash and you dry—how about that?" Lucas asked.

"You know, it's really not necessary." She should get him out of there. "I—"

"I insist."

Ivy just wanted him to leave. Her kitchen wasn't big enough for the burgeoning tension between them.

"You know where everything goes, so it makes sense," he said.

"Right."

They switched places so he could wash, and a few minutes in, he started making conversation. "So what do you do for fun?"

"What do you mean?"

"What do you do? Seems like you're always here with Katie."

"I'm not. I have a life outside of Katie." She rinsed a plate under the water and then started drying it.

"I'm sure you do. Do you go out a lot?"

"Not much. Every now and again."

"You dating anyone?"

She slanted a look at him. "What do you care? Don't you have your women?" Why had she brought that up? She sounded jealous even to her own ears.

"It's not an indictment, Ivy. It's just a question."

In other words, she shouldn't be so sensitive. "I don't date much, but I have."

"Seeing anyone in particular?"

"I have friends."

He stopped washing the bowl in his hands. "Friends? Friends with benefits—plural?"

"Maybe. I don't know. It's awkward for me to have this conversation with you."

"Why?"

"Because we have history."

He chuckled. "Ancient history. What, you think I'm going to be jealous or something?" He began washing again.

His comment pained her. When he said it like that, it did seem ridiculous. Just because she had remnants of feelings for him, didn't mean he cared one way or the other about her. "You would have to care to be jealous." She dried the white bowl they'd served the salad in.

"Who says I don't." Her pulsed jumped in response to the quietly spoken words. She turned in his direction; he was looking at her intently. "You're the mother of my daughter, and we have to get along. For Katie's sake."

Ivy let out the breath she didn't know she'd been holding. "Yes, for Katie's sake. She's the priority." Ivy would do well to remember that.

She opened the cabinet and reached toward the top shelf to put away the bowl.

"Let me get that for you," Lucas said.

"I've got it. I'll use the stool."

He wouldn't listen, though, and before she could move, he was already behind her.

"No need," he said. She felt the heat from him. Or had her body turned into an oven because he stood so close?

"I can get it," Ivy said almost in a panic.

He took the bowl. "I'm taller and I have a longer reach." He set it on the top shelf where it belonged. She held her breath as his hips brushed her backside and closed her eyes against the sensations twisting through her.

She clutched the counter and stayed perfectly still, waiting for him to move. He didn't, and his warm breath fanned the back of her hair.

"What are you doing?" she asked.

He didn't answer. He traced his hand down her arm and she jerked away from his touch. His fingertips had been so light, barely there, but she felt the sensations *everywhere.*

"Still don't want me to touch you?"

When she didn't answer, he brushed her hair out of the way to expose her nape. His mouth pressed against the back of her neck, the soft hairs of his beard caressing her sensitive skin. A whimper escaped her lips.

"Is it because you hate it, or because you like it too much? Which is it, Ivy?"

She curled her fingers into her palms on the counter. Maybe if she didn't react he would stop.

"Still don't want me to touch you?" His tongue flicked at the shell of her ear. "Look at me." She didn't turn. She was afraid to. "Look at me."

A soft, deep-throated chuckle warmed her skin. He turned her in his arms.

"What's wrong?"

"Lucas, this is a mistake, and you know it." That beautiful mouth of his was so close. Only inches away.

"Kissing you wouldn't be a mistake, Ivy. You may think so, but I don't."

Then his head swooped down and he crushed his mouth to hers.

CHAPTER FOURTEEN

The kiss was so sudden it took Ivy by surprise. She gripped his powerful triceps as he applied pressure to her spine, flattening her against him. Combined with the freshness of the cinnamon mints, the heady taste of him filled her mouth.

She could no longer think. The touch of his lips sent shudders zigzagging through her. He lowered his hand to splay across her bottom and pulled her in tighter. She felt every inch of his hard, aroused body. Desire throbbed between her legs, making her panties damp. She softened, practically melting into him, her nipples hardening in anticipation of more.

"Goddamn," he groaned. He reached his tongue between her lips to taste deep into her mouth. With a helpless sigh of pleasure, she opened to him.

She trembled in the circle of his arms and rubbed her hips against his crotch, eliciting a deep-chested groan that resounded in her own chest. His hand gripped one of her butt cheeks and squeezed, and she felt the sensual thrust of his hard length in her abdomen as he rotated his pelvis. When she gasped, he released her mouth and dragged his teeth along her chin and down her throat. He bit her neck and sucked hard against the skin of her collarbone. He knew that was her spot. It turned her into an overly-aroused prisoner of lust.

His other hand fisted in her hair and tugged, yanking the strands against her scalp. His treatment of her could be deemed too rough, but it wasn't. She enjoyed the pain with the pleasure. His aggressive passion had driven her out of her mind years ago. He'd marked her on more than one occasion, his coarse handling leaving bruises on her skin. His tutelage had awakened a brazenness, a hunger not evident in her before she met him. He'd taught her more about her body and sexuality than any book or magazine.

She reached between them and skated her hand up his jeans. Shivers raced down her spine as she cupped him in her hand. He groaned, gyrating against her palm in time to her ardent caress.

"You want this," he said. Not a question, a statement of fact.

"Yes," she admitted, her voice husky and trembling with desire. She could hardly breathe from the unexpected need. She wanted to drop to her knees and fill her mouth with him. She wanted to suck and pull until he unleashed into the back of her throat and she could have the pleasure once again of tasting him in the most intimate of ways.

The carnal nature of her thoughts shocked her. Ivy froze in the midst of their passionate episode. Reality returned with a vengeance, and she sprang back, tearing out of Lucas's arms.

He stared at her in surprise, chest heaving, body obviously going through the same tumultuous experience as hers. What she couldn't figure out was how the snap on his jeans had come undone. Who had opened it?

Her fingers trembled.

Had she been so impatient for a taste of him she'd undone the snap herself?

Ivy put a hand over her face and took a deep breath. "That shouldn't have happened." She swallowed. "We can't do this. We can't sleep together."

"Why not?" he asked. His breathing sounded shallow and harsh.

"If things—we—don't work out, it becomes a problem."

"If that's the only reason, then—"

"No, it's not the only reason." She fought the trembling that threatened to overtake her entire body. "I don't want to be your plaything, someone you use to pass the time with. I know you, Lucas. It's been a long time, but you're still pretty much the same man. I dragged you into the fatherhood role, and maybe you're getting comfortable with it, but you're not the settling down type. I'm not looking for anything casual, and certainly not with you."

His head jerked back as if she'd struck him. "What do you mean, certainly not with me?"

She dragged her tongue across her lips. God, she could still taste him. She still ached for him, and if he pushed, she didn't think she could resist. "We have history, and we already know we can't work. We want different things in a relationship. If you need to have your sexual needs satisfied, you'll have to go elsewhere."

"So you want to pretend there's nothing between us?" He sounded incredulous.

"If we ignore it, it—whatever *it* is—will eventually go away."

"You know what *it* is, and you don't believe that for one second." His eyes challenged hers.

"You don't live in Seattle. What would be the point?"

He ran his hand over his head in frustration. "So we behave as if there's no attraction between us? That's damn near impossible. I don't see how you expect me to do that."

"You'll have to figure it out."

"Yeah." He gave a mirthless laugh. He eyed her with animosity, as if he was angry that he still wanted her so much.

She forced herself to say the words that would bring her peace of mind. "You should go."

"Ivy—"

"Please." She hadn't meant to beg, but what was happening between them was more than she could handle.

He didn't move, and for a moment she thought he would persist, but then with one last look at her, Lucas left the kitchen and she followed. He strode through the condo and closed the front door behind him without so much as a good-bye. He gave her what she wanted, but it didn't make her happy at all. Because having him leave wasn't what she wanted. She wanted him.

All of a sudden, the door swung open and Lucas charged back in. She heard words that sounded something like "One last time," before he grabbed her into a long, devouring kiss that robbed the breath from her lungs. Tilting his head to the side, he plundered her mouth and pushed her against the wall. He trapped her hands on either side of her head and took his fill. For the second time that night, nothing else existed but him. He surrounded her, his scent, his muscular body. Long fingers bit into her wrists and the firm pressure of his mouth stripped her of resistance.

Caught in the grip of an unholy lust, she humped his thigh

between her legs. He kissed her harder and she strained closer, returning his ardor despite herself. When he finally tore his mouth away, his harsh breath warmed her cheek as he kissed her jaw. He attacked her throat with open-mouthed kisses and went lower. His lips grazed the ripe buds of her nipples beneath her shirt, and the faint touch provoked a helpless whimper she couldn't stop even if she'd tried. He gave one long, provocative tug on her nipple between his teeth before he lifted his head to look into her eyes.

His lids were at half-mast, but she saw the tempest brewing in the depths of his dilated pupils. His warm breath fanned her lips, which burned from the bruising power of his kiss.

"I'll do what you ask, Ivy, but I want to make love to you. I've been wanting to since I saw you at the anniversary party, and that's not going to change." His lips grazed hers. "You and I both know how good it is between us. I haven't forgotten, and I'm sure you haven't, either. I'll respect your request, but know that I don't like it one bit." He ground his hips against hers so she could feel his hard-on. She inhaled sharply and closed her eyes. "I'll do my best to be good, but I'm no saint. I hope you understand how hard it's going to be to keep my goddamn hands off of you."

He planted one last kiss on her mouth and stroked the interior with his tongue. Then suddenly he was gone. As the door swung closed behind him, he called out, "Lock the door behind me."

It wasn't a casual, meaningless comment. His words predicted danger to come if she didn't adhere to his instructions. Ivy moved on legs that barely allowed her to stand, much less walk.

"Lock the door!" he hollered out in the hall.

With a surge of vigor, she scrambled for the latch and twisted the dead bolt into place.

****

The next few days were hard, but Lucas continued to visit because his desire to bond with Katie was greater than his need to avoid Ivy and the attraction between them. They maneuvered around each other easily enough, but the ever-present tension created an invisible boundary. One that, in his opinion, felt tenuously thin. Being around her and having to pretend not to notice her every move was a near impossible feat to accomplish. They circled each other, careful not to touch or say the wrong thing. It had him on edge.

On the plus side, he and his daughter grew closer. So close, he didn't experience a lick of shame when he questioned Katie the day they went to the park. They'd been there all morning, with him chasing Katie around, listening to her high-pitched squeals of laughter and regretting that in a couple of days he'd be on a plane back to Georgia and didn't know when he'd be able to come out to see her again.

He was pushing her on the swing and Ivy had settled onto a bench nearby when a man with dark—almost black—skin walked up to Ivy. She stood up immediately and gave him a big hug, and he lifted her off her feet in the middle of the embrace. They settled into conversation, but what caught Lucas's eye was that the man didn't quite release her. They knew each other well, or at least he guessed they did by the familiar way the man touched her. The arm around her waist fell away, but the other lingered on her arm. Since she didn't move away, his touch clearly didn't bother her.

"Who's that man with your mom?" Lucas asked.

Katie craned her neck in their direction. "That's Mr. Gil. He's Mommy's friend. He's nice. He gave her flowers on her birthday."

So who was this Gil character? One of her friends with benefits?

Lucas sized him up; hard to do from that distance. He had longish dark hair and wore a gold loop earring. He was casually but sharply dressed in a sports jacket over dark jeans. From this vantage point, Lucas couldn't quite tell his ethnicity, but he could tell the guy was good-looking.

He continued to watch the exchange.

"Higher," Katie whined.

Lucas shifted his attention back to his daughter. He'd been so caught up in watching Ivy and her friend he'd all but stopped pushing Katie. He returned to the task at hand, keeping watch from the corner of his eye until the man left.

Minutes after he did Katie grew tired of the swing, and they made their way over to the bench.

"Who wants ice cream?" Ivy asked.

"Ice cream, yay!" Katie said, clapping her hands rapidly in a show of excitement.

Ivy smiled at Lucas, but the expression died on her face when their eyes met. "Is something wrong?"

"Nothing's wrong. Just wondering who that man was."

"Who, Gil?" She laughed easily. "He's a friend."

"You can't be too careful. You know, since you have a daughter."

She seemed startled by his suggestion that Gil would do anything to harm Katie. "You don't have to worry about Gil. He's a good person. Come on, munchkin. Let's go get some ice cream."

Katie skipped along beside her mother and Lucas followed more slowly. How close was Ivy with this Gil character, and were there others like him in her life, lurking in the wings? How many of them had Katie met, and did she enjoy their company?

The thought of a stream of men coming in and out of their lives soured his stomach.

Next week, he would be back in Georgia, but Gil would still be here. He didn't like the thought of some man hanging around. It made him uneasy. He and his daughter were getting closer. In fact, the last couple of times he'd arrived at the condo, she'd given him a big hug, clearly happy to see him.

Yet there was a noticeable thing missing from their relationship. Something he needed. Reassurance, against what he wasn't sure.

Katie hadn't called him daddy yet. She hadn't called him anything.

CHAPTER FIFTEEN

Ivy's mother wanted to meet Lucas, and whatever Constance Johnson wanted, she received. Despite Ivy's reservations, she could no longer put off introducing him to her family. No doubt he would undergo severe scrutiny, not so much from her mother, but from her brothers, Cyrus and Trenton.

Her mother had invited them to Sunday dinner, a formal affair that had to be taken very seriously. As children, they didn't always eat dinner at the table as a family, but Sunday meals were the exception. After services at St. Mark's Episcopal Church, the seven of them gathered in the formal dining room. Sometimes they invited guests, but most of the time it was an opportunity to bond as a family, and no discussions about beer-making or the restaurant business were allowed.

During these meals, Ivy and her brothers learned their family history. Constance Newton had been a Texas socialite when introduced to Cyrus Senior on his visit to Houston with his father. Under the guise of needing financial backing from Constance's father to open a new restaurant in the area, the two young people had been introduced. However, it soon became obvious their parents had arranged the meeting to get them together, and fortunately, they'd hit it off.

The marriage of Constance Newton and Cyrus Johnson merged two wealthy families whose lineage could be traced back hundreds of years. The Newtons' ancestors were among the first free blacks that settled on the continent, ending their servitude as indentured servants before the economics of slavery proved too lucrative an enterprise to resist. As such, they built their wealth through the acquisition of land. Ultimately they thrived by offering banking and insurance services to blacks who couldn't get them elsewhere, and Constance's family eventually moved to Texas where she was born.

The Johnsons could trace their roots to the U.S. Virgin Islands. Before the United States bought the islands, the Danish had owned them, and in 1848 the Danes freed all the slaves in the territory, a full fifteen years before the Emancipation Proclamation in the United States. Cyrus Johnsons' ancestors had been an enterprising lot and started several businesses in the islands, but they earned their wealth in the food industry. Moving to the United States, they opened restaurants in the north, affording blacks the opportunity to dine in establishments similar to the ones they would normally be turned away from. It grew into a multi-million dollar business that touched almost every state in the country.

Years later, Cyrus Senior expanded his family's business into a conglomerate. He included beer making and converted the restaurants into The Brew Pub, to capitalize on the popularity of the beer.

Today, Ivy's mother lived in a gorgeous six bedroom estate on Lake Washington, a large freshwater lake a short drive from Seattle. Her mother had downsized to the property a few years after Cyrus Senior passed away. In addition to the main house, the expansive grounds featured a playground for Katie, a boat house, two docks, and a guest house where the family housekeeper, Adelina, lived. The stately home contained an indoor swimming pool, a library, a wine cellar, and her mother had commissioned a state-of-the-art movie lounge where she watched her favorite old movies on a theater-size screen.

Lucas had insisted on driving rather than having Lloyd drive, so he and Ivy sat in the front and Katie rode in the back. Her daughter prattled on about her grandmother, the playground, and feeding the ducks. Lost in her own thoughts, Ivy kept her eyes glued to the passing scenery.

Ever since Lucas had questioned her about Gil, she had been a little more cautious around him. She didn't know if jealousy or true concern for Katie's safety prompted his comment about Gil, but she'd decided to refrain from mentioning him in future to keep the peace.

Even if he was jealous, marriage was not on his list of things to do. He'd told her so as recently as the day he'd arrived unexpectedly to her office. But that's what she was holding out for. She'd seen the affectionate, loving relationship her parents shared and wanted the same. She wanted it all, right down to the mundane tasks of washing dishes together or—out of the corner of her eye she hazarded a glance at Lucas in the driver's seat—sitting around doing crossword puzzles until their daughter fell asleep.

She repressed a sigh. Lucas didn't want any of that. Just like he'd told her he didn't want children. He was only with them now because she'd taken that choice away from him, and it would be good to remember that and not get any fanciful ideas.

The minute they entered the formal foyer, her mother came out to greet them. She was an attractive woman with a standing weekly appointment at the salon to keep her shoulder length coif styled and free of gray hairs. She often gave her age as fifty, even though she'd surpassed that milestone years ago.

She reminded Ivy of a ballerina, gliding around on the tips of her feet in pointy-toed stilettoes that might have been more appropriate for a younger woman, but that she was completely at ease in. If you could tell how a woman would age by looking at her mother, Ivy was fortunate to come from this particular gene pool.

"Grandma!" Katie ran to her grandmother and flung her arms around her waist.

Constance cupped her granddaughter's face. "Hello, Katherine. How are you?" Ivy's mother never used nicknames.

"Fine. I'm starving."

"You're always hungry, aren't you?" Constance teased. She lifted curious eyes to Lucas. "Welcome to my home."

"Thank you."

"May I call you Lucas?"

"Absolutely." He started forward.

"And you may call me Constance." She met him halfway, but when he extended his hand to her, the perfectly arched brow above her left eye winged upward. "I give hugs to family, Lucas, and since you're Katherine's father, I consider you family."

Ivy appreciated the welcome her mother extended. She watched her mother envelope Lucas in one of her firm embraces. When she was done, she turned to Ivy.

"Hello, Mother."

"Good to see you, dear." Ivy and her mother hugged and exchanged air kisses.

"This way." Constance placed her hand in the crook of Lucas's arm—her way of helping him feel at ease and letting the rest of the household know she welcomed him and they should be on their best behavior.

They entered the spacious sitting room. A grand piano that no one played sat in a corner between two large windows. Trenton and Cyrus were already in there, standing by the fireplace with drinks in their hands and talking. When they walked in, her brothers looked up and fixed Lucas with the type of stare usually reserved for animals at a zoo. She wondered if he felt that way, like a curiosity put on display for spectators.

Cyrus and Trenton approached and shook his hand. Cyrus's face maintained the usual rigid lines, as if his jaw would hurt if he dared crack a smile. Trenton at least fixed his face into a more friendly expression, although his eyes remain guarded.

After the introductions, Adelina, their housekeeper, appeared in the doorway. She and Constance had grown up in the same household together in Texas and Adelina was more of a friend than an employee. When Constance had moved to Seattle as a new wife, she'd asked Adelina to come with her and help her run her new household.

"Dinner is almost ready," Adelina said, her voice accented with a hint of her Mexican roots.

"Since we have a little time, I'm going to borrow Ivy for a few minutes," Cyrus announced. Before Ivy could agree or disagree, he drew her from the room with a firm hand clasped below her elbow. She felt the weight of their mother's disapproving frown as they exited the room.

"Mother's going to kill you," Ivy said. "What's so important you couldn't wait until after dinner?"

They entered the library, a place filled with books their father had collected over the years. Many first editions, some worth well into the thousands of dollars, lined the shelves or lay encased in protective glass.

Without a word, Cyrus handed her a file.

"What's this?" Ivy asked.

"I looked into Lucas Baylor."

Although she wasn't surprised her brother had done a background check, it still annoyed her. "I asked you not to meddle."

"Did you really think I'd welcome him into the family without checking him out first?"

"We can't unwelcome him. He's Katie's father," she reminded him.

"We should at least know what and who we're dealing with."

"You need a life, Cyrus."

"Let's not make this about me. Open it."

Ivy perused the file, and he continued talking. "Did you know he was part of the foster system for years? He got into all sorts of trouble—fighting, stealing, and he almost flunked out of school. He was a real juvenile delinquent."

Ivy looked up from the second page, which contained information about Lucas's height, weight, even down to his shoe size. Cyrus's guy was very thorough.

"Yes, I know all about his past. He was abandoned at Grady Hospital in Atlanta. They estimated he was a year old at the time, but they don't know for sure. He doesn't know who he is. He doesn't know who his parents are or why they left him. He doesn't know his real name. He doesn't know his birthday—doesn't even celebrate it because obviously he doesn't know when it is. Yes, he had some bad behavior, but he straightened out in high school."

Cyrus actually appeared speechless, which was a first.

"Did you know all of this when you became involved with him?"

"Some of it I learned afterward, but for the most part, yes." She didn't know what that had to do with anything.

"Why do you do this, Ivy?" He sounded annoyed with her.

"Do what?" She slammed the file closed.

"Get involved with men who are no good for you?"

"That's not what you mean. Don't you mean not good enough for you?"

"This isn't about me."

"You're sure? Because you seem very interested in my personal life right now." He always had been, particularly after "the incident."

"To protect you."

"Thanks, but I don't need protecting." She appreciated his

concern, but Cyrus's overbearing, big brother routine drove her crazy.

"All I'm saying is, be careful," he said. "When people find out the truth, that you lied and let another man raise Katie as his own, they may not look too favorably on you."

She knew that and had thought about it for days. "They're going to eventually find out. We can't keep this a secret forever, and frankly, I don't think it'll be as catastrophic as you think. I had Katie eight years ago, and Winston's been dead for two. People don't care as much as you think they do."

"I disagree. As much as possible we've cultivated a private and scandal-free life, but there's bound to be a media firestorm when it gets out that Winston wasn't Katie's father. That while you were supposedly engaged to him, you became pregnant with another man's child."

Aside from Jim Koch of Samuel Adams, the average consumer didn't know who owned the company that made their favorite beer. Being black billionaires and running such a large, privately-owned brewing company, the Johnsons tended to make the news whether they wanted to or not. They were a novelty, which made people curious about their lives.

"It's ancient history," Ivy pushed back, wanting to believe this entire issue was a nonissue and ignore Cyrus's prediction of doom.

"Listen to me," Cyrus said, "I'm not saying all of this to scare you, but after what happened last time, we can't be too careful."

Why did he have to bring that up? "I was *seventeen*, Cyrus. I made a mistake."

Her involvement with Eric Atkerson had been the biggest mistake she'd ever made and caused more drama than she cared to remember. He'd been a sophomore attending the University of Washington on a basketball scholarship, and she'd lied about her age, telling him she was eighteen when she was only seventeen. Getting involved with him had been an act of rebellion. She and her friends had wanted to be bad, cool—whatever young girls wanted at that age, and Eric had a dangerous edge and a roughness about him she wasn't accustomed to from the boys at her prep school. He offered the right amount of excitement to make her young heart race and keep her coming back for more.

She allowed him to video tape them having sex. He'd promised it was for their eyes only and no one else would see it, and she'd believed him. It had been a disastrous mistake. Eric tried to shop the film, but because of her age, no one would touch it. The family lawyers easily suppressed its distribution, but it still made the rounds.

To know a video had circulated online and remained dormant in computer caches and hidden in the archives of cell phones still managed to make Ivy feel queasy. Most of her friends had distanced themselves after the story came out, but Winston had been one of the few who'd remained loyal during the entire ordeal.

Cyrus and her brothers had closed rank immediately. Trenton had been too young to participate in the retaliation, but Gavin, Cyrus, and Xavier wasted no time finding Eric and they let Gavin—the wild one, who wanted to handle this himself for his twin—whoop his ass. They forced him to apologize to Ivy, but the damage had been done.

The media had had a field day, linking the evils of beer with what they called her "wild child antics." There had even been speculation that she'd been drunk when she shot the video, and those rumors had taken on a life of their own. She'd been likened to a drug pusher, encouraging underage drinking among her friends, though nothing could be further from the truth.

Except for the beat down, Eric came out of the entire ordeal practically unscathed, but her reputation had been in a shambles. She'd been called a whore, that word being the least derogatory of some of the name-calling. The International Debutante Ball in New York rescinded her invitation. Her aunt had managed to wrangle the invite, using all of her connections and calling in favors to ensure Ivy had the proper coming out. All had been for naught and the disappointment expressed by her aunt and her parents had been just as crushing as knowing she'd been used as a pawn in a cruel game.

To this day Ivy didn't think either of her parents knew the truth about her brothers' involvement in the retribution. Eric's parents had filed a civil lawsuit against the Johnsons, which had been tossed out of court for lack of evidence. Cyrus had been ruthlessly thorough. He'd hired ironclad alibis for him and his brothers before he planned the attack.

"Do you still have feelings for Lucas?" Cyrus asked.

"Cy—"

He swore and placed both hands on her shoulders. "Tell me the truth."

She sighed. She didn't want to discuss her feelings for Lucas. "I don't know what I feel. Mostly guilt that I've kept him and Katie apart for so long. Seeing them together and their closeness makes it worse. It's clear I made the wrong decision nine years ago."

"You made the best decision you could at the time, and you didn't make it on your own. We all did it with you."

Ivy held out the documents to him. "I don't need this."

"Keep it."

"I guess you already made a copy for yourself?"

"Don't I always?" He grinned sideways. He so rarely smiled, it surprised her. Why didn't he smile more? He should definitely smile more.

She tucked the file into her purse.

"Come on, let's go before Mother gets upset and castrates me for making her hold dinner for us," he said.

"She would never castrate you. You know you're her favorite because you remind her of dad."

He smiled again, which made her happy.

CHAPTER SIXTEEN

Lucas had the distinct impression Cyrus didn't like him. The guy looked at him as if he thought he'd run off with the silverware, and his distrust irked Lucas. He resigned himself to the thought that it was probably just brotherly protectiveness and focused on his surroundings.

Sunday dinner at the Johnsons was quite the affair. The servants served the meal in the formal dining room at a table that seated ten and had two chandeliers hanging overhead.

Constance sat at the head of the table. Lucas, Katie, and Ivy sat to her left, and Cyrus and Trenton across from them. The delicious feast started with a first course of white bean soup with wild mushrooms, followed by a mixed green salad with apples and what tasted like homemade buttermilk dressing. The main entrée, a slow-roasted prime rib accompanied by roasted fingerling potatoes and candied carrots, practically melted in Lucas's mouth.

"Adelina's an excellent cook," he said halfway through the meal. Since he hadn't received the grilling he'd expected, he'd relaxed considerably.

"I don't know what I'd do without her," Constance said.

"Anybody home?" A male voice boomed from near the front of the house, and everyone looked up from their plates.

"Uncle Xavier!" Katie said in an excited whisper. She rushed out of the room, followed by the rest of the family. Lucas pulled up the rear in time to see his daughter leap into her uncle's arms.

Lucas remembered Ivy talking about her older brother, the one right behind Cyrus, but Xavier Johnson was not what he expected. The more he learned about this family, the more he recognized the uniqueness of each member. The way he was dressed, no one would ever guess Xavier was worth billions. A red, gold, and green dashiki covered the upper half of his tall frame, and a pair of worn jeans encased his legs. He had a head full of dreadlocks pulled back from his face and secured with a leather strap. He'd dropped an olive-green army duffel bag to the floor when Katie ran to him.

"You've gotten big," he said. "I can barely lift you."

Katie giggled. "What did you bring me?"

"Nothing. Except this." Xavier pulled out a small figurine, ash gray in color.

Katie took it from him. "What is it?"

"It's called the 'Thinking Man.' I thought it would be perfect for my very smart niece. It's made of Kisii stone."

Katie ran her fingers lightly over the abstract design. "Kisii stone," she repeated.

"That's right. It's named after the Kisii tribe in Kenya. They hand carve all kinds of objects, but I thought this one would be perfect for you. Take good care of it, okay?"

"I will," Katie said solemnly. Lucas knew she would by the way she clutched the object to her chest.

Xavier let her slide down and his eyes swept over his family. They rested briefly on Lucas, a question in them before he embraced Trenton, Adelina, Ivy, and then his mother. The hugs he gave the women lasted much longer, and they clearly enjoyed them, laying their heads against his chest with smiles of contentment on their faces.

Constance patted his cheek. "It's good to have you home."

She turned around and introduced Lucas. When Lucas shook Xavier's hand, he noted not only the strength in his handshake but the roughness of his hands, verifying he was no pampered billionaire. He worked with his hands and worked hard.

If Xavier was surprised to learn Katie's real father had shown up for dinner, he didn't let on. "Welcome," he said to Lucas.

"I'm surprised I got the opportunity to meet you," Lucas said. "From what I understand, your work keeps you in Africa most of the time." Xavier was an ambassador of sorts, working with various nonprofit organizations. They brought attention to the plight of

Africans in underdeveloped regions and shined the spotlight on how the continent's resources were being exploited without the financial benefits trickling down to ordinary citizens.

"Usually," Xavier confirmed, "but I have to come home every now and again to spend time with the family."

"Every time you come home you're so skinny," Adelina said, shaking her head.

"I don't have access to your delicious meals over there." Xavier patted his stomach. "Something smells good, though, and I'm tired of eating antelope."

Katie gasped, eyes wide. "Antelope?"

"Yeah, it's good, but after a while, it gets old."

"What does it taste like?" she asked.

He paused, screwing his face into an exaggerated scowl of deep thought. "You know, it tastes like chicken."

"No it doesn't!" She laughed.

"You have not been eating antelope," Trenton said with a shake of his head. "Every time you come back you've got a crazy story to tell."

Xavier looped his arms around his mother and Ivy. "Sure I have. Away from the city, we eat whatever's available, and antelope was available in abundance."

"What else did you eat?" Katie asked, walking backward so she wouldn't miss a word as they made their way to the dining room.

"Depends on where we were. Sometimes fruit, other times bugs."

Katie's eyes widened. "Really?"

Xavier shrugged. "Sometimes that's all we had. Other times we'd go hunting and roast whatever we could find. Sometimes we ate rattlesnake, sometimes anteaters."

Katie wrinkled her nose. "What does anteater taste like?"

"Katherine dear," Constance said, "we'll save the conversation about bugs and anteaters until after dinner, okay?"

"Okay, Grandma."

"I'll tell you everything you need to know when we're done with Adelina's good food," Xavier promised with a wink.

They were back in the dining room, and it was then that Lucas noticed Cyrus had remained seated at the table. He was the only one who hadn't gone out to welcome his brother home. The two men barely looked at each other as Xavier sat down beside Lucas.

"How long are you staying this time?" Ivy asked.

"About a month or so. If that's all right." He looked at his mother.

"You know you're always welcome." The pleased expression on her face left no doubt of her sincerity.

Adelina placed a table setting in front of Xavier. "You all right, bro?" he asked.

Cyrus sliced into his prime rib. He placed the morsel into his mouth and calmly chewed. "Perfect. You?"

It was impossible to miss the tension that descended on the room.

"Boys," Constance said.

"I'm good, Mother," Xavier said. "I suspect my dear brother would have preferred if I were eaten by a lion out on the plains."

"We can't always have what we want," Cyrus said.

"Enough," Constance said. "Not at my dinner table and not while there's a child present."

Cyrus continued, as if his mother hadn't spoken. "Isn't it great how some of us can go gallivanting around the world while the rest of us stay here and work our butts off?"

"Because what I do isn't important?" Xavier demanded. Seated beside him, Lucas felt the coiled tension. "Bringing attention to the underprivileged and marginalized of the world isn't work? Because you can't see a return on investment on a financial statement for the work I do, that makes it irrelevant?"

"Xavier, Cyrus, please," Ivy begged.

Trenton didn't say a word, choosing instead to watch his brothers, his gaze lobbing back and forth between them like he was watching a tennis match. Adelina stepped back from the table with her arms crossed in front of her as if she expected an explosion to erupt at any minute.

"I know you think you're some kind of hero," Cyrus said, "but running from your responsibilities doesn't make you a hero. It makes you a coward."

Xavier shot up from his chair.

Cyrus paused with a fingerling potato in the prongs of the fork halfway to his mouth. He didn't flinch. "I dare you," he said.

"Xavier, sit down!" Constance's voice sounded shrill and strained.

Xavier's chest heaved as he tried to regain control. He shot daggers at Cyrus, and for a split second Lucas wondered if he'd ignore his mother's command and leap across the table. No one moved, and after a long, taut silence, he slowly lowered into the chair.

Constance set her hands on the table and took a deep breath of relief. "I need the two of you to act like you have some sense, instead of like a bunch of uncivilized ruffians. *Not at my dinner table.*"

The dynamics of this family were getting more and more interesting. Lucas didn't know what the hell was going on between Cyrus and Xavier, but whatever it was, the animosity ran deep. Constance placed a hand over her heart, as if her outburst had expended all her energy.

"We have a guest," she continued. "And there is a child present."

Katie clutched the Thinking Man replica, her little shoulders slumped, eyes trained on the plate in front of her. Ivy rubbed her back to comfort her, but the joy of seeing her uncle had long passed and been replaced by the discomfort palpable in the air.

"Adelina," Constance said.

The housekeeper rushed forward. "Yes, Mrs. Johnson."

"Please go ahead and serve Xavier."

"Yes, Mrs. Johnson."

Constance cleared her throat and smiled at Lucas. "Ivy said you're a writer, and you offer relationship advice?"

Lucas nodded, wondering where the conversation was headed now that the tension in the room had calmed to a degree. One of the servants leaned over his shoulder and refilled his water glass.

"You're an expert on women?"

He laughed. "No, and I don't pretend to be. I'm an expert on men, because I'm a man and I understand how men think."

"Surely you're not saying all men are the same?" Constance sipped her wine.

Feeling all eyes on him, Lucas chose his words carefully. His typically blunt, in-your-face answers wouldn't work here. "Not at all, but there are commonalities among us. To be honest, most of the advice I offer has more to do with how a particular woman might allow a man to treat her, thinking that somehow hanging in there or putting up with bad behavior would make a man love her. When really, it won't."

"Perhaps you can offer advice to the young women Trenton dates," Constance said, casting a reproving look in her son's direction.

All eyes turned to Trenton, who paused with his drink halfway to his mouth. "I don't date. I have hook-ups," he said.

"Language, Trenton," his mother warned.

"Sorry, Mother." He smiled broadly and looked completely unrepentant. He turned to Lucas and shifted the conversation back to him. "Do you ever have problems with the advice you offer?"

"Not often. Every now and again someone will write an article lashing out at me and my advice, but as my publicist always says, even bad publicity is good publicity."

"Not for us," Cyrus stated. "Bad publicity is bad publicity."

Lucas sensed the change in the air. While he courted the media, this family didn't. Intensely private, they wanted the emphasis to be on their restaurants and beer, but the reporters were always on the look out for scandalous stories.

Silence fell over the table, and only the sound of silverware clanking against the fine china could be heard. From the corner of his eye, he saw Ivy focused on her meal. Did his comment bring up painful memories? While he'd threatened her with revealing her wrongdoing to the press, in truth he wouldn't have done it. By her own recounting of the story years ago, he knew how much she'd suffered as a teen from the sex tape fiasco.

"I did have one situation with a male reader a couple of years ago," Lucas said, in an effort to lighten the room. "A man stood up at one of my workshops and accused me of being a no-name charlatan who didn't have the credentials to offer counsel to anyone. He accused me of capitalizing on women's fears and asked everyone present to ignore me and tell their friends to do the same. Then he made a pitch for his own book and rattled off a list of certifications and degrees that he said made him way more qualified than I was to offer relationship advice. He struck me as the kind of man who thinks the sun comes up just to hear him crow."

Constance set her fork down. "My goodness, I haven't heard that saying in a long time. My grandmama used to say that about people she thought were cocky." She laughed quietly to herself, as if reminiscing about the past.

"I've got plenty more where that came from. I used to tell them to Ivy all the time."

"Yes, you did," Ivy said. A smile touched her lips.

Constance watched the exchange between them with a raised

brow. "How did you handle the interruption from the audience member?"

"I told him this wasn't the time or place for an advertisement and if he wanted to talk, we could do it after the event."

"That was nice of you, considering he interrupted your workshop," Constance said.

"Well," Lucas said, "my mama used to tell me, 'Keep calm, say what you have to say, and move on. Don't argue with idiots. They'll drag you down and beat you with experience every time.'"

Constance laughed out loud and covered her mouth. For a second Lucas saw Ivy in her, the unabashed amusement, the eyes sparkling in her face. An uncanny resemblance, right down to covering her mouth with her hand.

Everyone else at the table laughed, too.

His gaze met Ivy's over Katie's head, and he read the unspoken message in her smile. He had more road to travel to be completely accepted by the family, but he'd already passed the first test.

CHAPTER SEVENTEEN

Lucas inhaled deeply of the nighttime air. He'd been back in Atlanta for a few weeks and stood with his arms folded on the railing of the balcony of his high-rise condo in Midtown. Living in this part of town embodied everything he appreciated about the single life in the city. Within walking distance he had his pick of restaurants, nightclubs, and single, independent women no more interested in getting hitched than he was.

Many stories below, traffic moved along at a steady pace with the occasional car honking and pedestrians hurrying along to get home or to dine at one of the restaurants lining the avenue.

Priscilla's arms wrapped around his waist from behind, and her warm cheek pressed against his bare back. "Sorry for the interruption earlier, but being the maid of honor is like being a doctor on call. I have to be available to handle all kinds of bridal emergencies."

Lucas felt pretty sure 'bridal emergencies' were being unsuitably compared to medical emergencies, but he refrained from voicing his opinion. Priscilla took her duties very seriously and he didn't want to belittle her role in her sister's wedding.

"When's the wedding again?" he asked.

She lifted her head from his back. "Do I need to enter the date into your phone? It's an evening ceremony the first Friday in December. You haven't forgotten, have you?"

Not a chance, since she'd brought it up several times. "I haven't forgotten, but I wanted to make sure I had the date right."

"Good." She tightened her arms around him. "What's going on, baby?" she asked. "You've been so distracted since you came back."

"Have I?"

"Yes, you're here, but you're not here. You're not yourself."

"I've got a lot on my mind." A light breeze blew across his skin. The September air wasn't quite chilly yet. Somewhere between warm and cool, it was the perfect temperature. It was ten degrees cooler in Seattle. He knew because he'd checked as he fiddled with his phone earlier, wondering what Ivy and Katie were doing, wondering if he should call again. Was he calling too much?

"Anything I can help with?" Priscilla rubbed his back.

"Nah." Her touch used to soothe him. Now it was a mild irritant.

"Come back to bed, then."

Lucas turned around and slipped an arm around her waist. "You go. I'm going to stay out here a little longer, okay?"

She pouted. "You sure I can't help?"

"It's nothing you can help me with. If you could, I promise I would tell you."

Priscilla sighed. "All right. I hope you're able to work out whatever's bothering you. I'm worried."

"Nothing to worry about."

Realizing she'd get nowhere with him, Priscilla pulled out of his arms. "Come back to bed soon, okay?" She squeezed his hand and then disappeared into the dark interior of the condo.

He felt a little guilty about the way he'd been distracted. After being on the road and spending those couple of weeks in Seattle, he'd been sure he would be ready to come home. Normally after an extended period away, he was. If he and Priscilla were back on, he welcomed her company. This time, though, he couldn't shake a restlessness he'd never experienced before.

He pulled his cellphone from his pocket and punched in the seven digits for Ivy's home in Seattle. It rang twice before she answered.

"Hi, Lucas," she greeted him. "You missed her. She went to bed early tonight."

Since he'd been back in town, calling and talking to Katie had become an almost nightly ritual. She told him about her day, her friends, and most of the time she did all the talking. All he had to do was listen, which was fine. Hearing her voice on a regular basis had become a welcome distraction from his nightly writing routine.

"That's too bad. How'd she do on the essay?"

"They haven't received their grades yet. Not until next week."

He and Ivy always spoke politely to each other, exchanging information rigidly restricted to their daughter and her activities. Keeping that in mind, he should wrap up the conversation.

"Was there something else?" Ivy asked, when the silence between them had drawn out to a longer than usual length of time.

"Not really. I…" Why was he trying to keep her on the phone? In the past few weeks, he really hadn't had much of a chance to talk to her, and right now he wasn't even sure why he wanted to.

"What are you doing?" he asked.

"Me?"

He smiled at the surprise in her voice. He leaned on the metal railing, relaxing into the conversation. "Yes, you."

"Oh…nothing really. I brought some work home and I'm doing it while I watch TV."

"You still watching those trashy shows?"

There was a short pause. "I plead the fifth."

"Come on, Ivy, I can't believe you're still addicted to reality shows." She used to make him watch them with her at his apartment. Then she'd spend half the time complaining to him about everyone's behavior.

"Don't judge me."

"How many of them are there now? Every time I turn around there's another one."

"I'm embarrassed to say I watch them, but it's nice to see other people have more problems than I do. It's like watching an accident on the highway and makes me realize how good my life is. That's bad, isn't it?"

"Yeah, that's pretty bad."

Another pause, another opportunity to end the call, but still he didn't. He could hear the television in the background, and then his mind went in a direction it shouldn't. He wondered if she was in bed, and what was she wearing if she was?

"Did I tell you that you turned into a really good cook?" he said.

"Really?" He heard the smile in her voice.

"Yeah, I have to give you credit, especially considering your limitations when we met." She'd definitely come a long way. He'd enjoyed the dinners at her place.

"Limitations. That's a nice way of putting it. The only time you got a meal from me was when I brought it home from a restaurant."

"It's the thought that counts."

"Next time you come, you'll have to cook," she told him.

"Deal. I know just the thing."

"Please tell me you have Mama Katherine's fried chicken recipe."

He chuckled. "It just so happens I do."

"Yes!"

He stood there, grinning like an idiot, but he couldn't stop. Hearing her voice just…did things to him.

"Remember when you bought me that silverware set?" he asked.

She laughed, the sound attractive and enticing. He looked down at his arms. Goose bumps had broken out on his flesh.

"Do I? It was an act of desperation. You only had three forks."

"I didn't need anymore than that."

"They come in packs of four."

"Yeah, well, I must have lost one at some point. I wasn't too worried about it. I appreciated you buying me a set, but you didn't have to."

"What choice did I have? I got tired of washing forks every time I wanted something to eat!"

They both broke into laughter at that. "Oh, so it's like that?"

"You brought it up," Ivy pointed out, when she finally caught her breath. Man, she had the best laugh, like she was all in on the joke. He wanted to immerse himself in the sound.

They grew quiet again, but this time the silence was less awkward and more from the reflection of shared memories.

"She misses you," Ivy said softly.

"She said that?"

"Pretty much. I didn't want to say anything, but she was crying in her room tonight. That's why she went to bed so early. She cried herself to sleep. She wanted to know why you can't live here like her first daddy."

Her voice thickened at the end, and Lucas felt his heart break a little bit. He bowed his head. "I…miss her, too." The words weren't as hard to say as he thought they'd be. What was hard was believing that he'd only known Katie for a short time.

"When are you coming back?" Ivy asked. Her voice sounded tentative, as if she didn't think she should even be asking such a question.

"In a couple of weeks."

He hadn't planned on flying back so soon, but knowing his daughter missed him, and knowing how he felt, he saw no reason to delay. He only had a couple of days of travel coming up, and the few deadlines he had to meet for *Ask Men* magazine and *Marie Claire* were ones he felt he could handle fairly quickly if he buckled down and put in longer hours. It was better to get in as many visits as he could before next year, when he would have less time because of his teaching schedule.

"You're coming back so soon?"

"I travel so much I have a lot of frequent flyer miles, so it's not a problem."

He heard Priscilla behind him as she came back to the patio door. "I thought you were coming back to bed," she said.

Lucas pulled the phone away from his ear and covered it to muffle the sound. He tried not to show his frustration when he looked at her. "I'll be there in a minute."

Her eyes dropped to the phone in his hand, her gaze accusatory. She made him feel guilty even though he wasn't doing anything wrong. He was having a perfectly innocent conversation.

With her face fixed into a mask of displeasure, Priscilla went back inside.

He lifted the phone to his ear again. "Hello?"

"I didn't know you had company," Ivy said.

Lucas rubbed the back of his head. "I do, but—"

"I'll let you go. I shouldn't have bothered you so late."

"*I* called *you*."

"I shouldn't keep you, then."

"You're not keeping me." A sense of desperation overcame him, as if something important was slipping away. It was just a conversation, but he needed to hold on a little bit longer and salvage the delicate rapport developing between them.

"Let me know when you'd like to come back."

"I'd like to—" The phone went dead, and he looked down at the screen in surprise.

Sighing, he stayed outside for a little longer, digesting the conversation, thinking about his daughter. Thinking about Ivy. Wondering what the hell was wrong with him and why he was thinking so much about Ivy. And what she was wearing. And how attractive her voice sounded when she talked, and her laugh—all warm and husky, and—

He was getting hard just thinking about her *laugh*.

He shook his head. He had to stop thinking about her because she'd made it clear she wanted nothing to do with him, and they weren't even on the same page when it came to relationships. His only concern should be for Katie, but Ivy filled his thoughts more and more often.

Maybe it was normal. After all, she was his daughter's mother. If he was honest with himself, he had to acknowledge something else was going on because he hadn't wanted to hang up. He'd wanted the conversation to go on for much longer. Even now, he was tempted to call back, but truthfully the moment, and whatever had transpired between them, had passed.

****

Ivy stared at the phone, barely holding back from tossing it across the room. But why punish the phone? It wasn't the phone's fault she had conveniently forgotten he was involved with other women. He certainly hadn't made a secret of his relationships. He'd told her from the beginning.

She was the one who'd lost sight of reality because he'd spoken to her in an overtly friendly way. It didn't help that she'd already gotten comfortable playing in her little fantasyland where she watched his and her daughter's bent heads as they worked on crossword puzzles. Or she cooked dinner and listened to them talking and giggling in the living room, and afterward Lucas would insist that since she'd cooked, he and Katie would clear the table and load the dishwasher. All of those little moments gave them more time together and more time to bond.

He had a woman at his place right now. She laughed bitterly as pain lanced through her chest. Of course he did. Lucas wouldn't be living his life like a monk.

The other day at work, Cynthia had told her she should date more, and her friend was right. She'd dated a little bit since Winston passed away, but she needed to really start dating. And she knew where to start.

She scrolled through the contacts in her phone and settled on a number. She hit send.

"Hello?"

Ivy smiled at his very proper British accent, one of his attractive qualities. She drew her legs up to her chest and settled back against the pillows. "Hi Gil, it's me, Ivy. It's not too late, is it?"

"I know it's you, and no, it's not too late. You know I'm a night owl. To what do I owe the pleasure?"

She felt better already. "When will you be back in the country?"

"In a couple of months or so," he replied.

"Do you still want to go out when you come back? If so, I'd like to take you up on your offer."

"Sounds like a smashing idea."

Ivy closed her eyes. Forget Lucas.

"Great," she said, keeping her voice upbeat. "Call me when you're back in Seattle."

CHAPTER EIGHTEEN

"Royal flush, gentlemen." Derrick laid his hand on the table, a wide grin plastered across his face.

"Dammit!" Lucas tossed down his cards and joined in the chorus of groans as his friend scraped his winnings to his side of the table.

Five of them had gathered to play poker in Derrick's man cave on the Saturday after Thanksgiving. In addition to Lucas, there was Derrick, Derrick's half brothers Roarke and Matthew, and their brother-in-law, Antonio.

After traveling to New York for an appearance that lasted Thanksgiving Day and the day after, Lucas came back to town and savored spending time with his buddies. The brothers often included him in family events—weddings, a bachelor party, or simply hanging out in Derrick's man cave, like they were tonight. They were the brothers he'd never had.

Located on the bottom floor of his mansion, Derrick's lair contained leather furniture and a polished steel, custom made pool table. A fully stocked bar and refrigerator ensured the men could eat and drink for hours without having to go upstairs. As if that wasn't enough, his chef had prepared platters of crab cakes, meatballs, a crazy-good hot caprese dip, and something called broccoli cheese bites that Lucas couldn't get enough of.

Tonight's get together had been prompted by his best friend Roarke's temporary return. A professor of physics at the University of Georgia, he was on loan to a university in Chile and had come home for the holidays. It was a one-year assignment, and he and his wife had decided that it was best to live apart for the year rather than uproot the entire family.

"This is ridiculous." Matthew scowled across the table at his brother. Derrick had won every single hand they'd played. He was definitely the better player amongst the five of them, but this was a record even for him.

Derrick chuckled. "Are you guys even playing?"

"I think you just invite us over to take our money," Lucas said, eyeing Derrick as he counted the cash.

Derrick laughed. "Sorry to have to do this to you again, gentlemen."

Antonio stood up from the table. "You're not sorry." He went over to the refrigerator and took out a beer.

"Don't you have enough money already?" Matthew asked Derrick.

"You can never have enough money, Matt," Derrick replied. His comment didn't come as a surprise to Lucas. Derrick had inherited millions from his adoptive father and strived to build the business left to him into an even bigger, more successful company.

"I'm done." Matthew scraped back his chair and went over to the pool table.

"Me, too." Antonio followed Matthew and they each grabbed a cue stick from the wall.

"Don't be sore losers," Derrick called, a grin on his face.

Roarke rose from the table and headed toward the bar. "I know you're cheating, but I haven't figured out how. Anybody else want a beer?" he asked.

"I'll take one," Lucas replied.

Roarke came back with two bottles of Full Moon beer. "I'm going to figure out how you're doing it, too," he said to Derrick.

"Did it ever occur to you that I might be a better player?" Derrick asked, his blue-gray eyes filled with amusement.

"No!" Matthew and Antonio yelled from across the room.

"I don't know if that's up for debate, since I'm the only one who won any hands tonight." Derrick was enjoying rubbing it in. The brothers went back and forth, taking verbal shots at each other for a while.

When they were done giving each other a hard time, Derrick turned in Lucas's direction. "You're quieter than usual," he observed.

"Thinking, man, just thinking." Something he'd been doing a lot of lately. He'd found it particularly hard to leave Seattle after his last trip. Katie's sad little face still haunted him.

"How are you adjusting to being a father?"

"I gotta hear this," Matthew called from across the room, "because I never expected you of all people would ever have kids."

Lucas snorted. "I didn't either, but I had one eight years ago." He launched into the story of his relationship with Ivy. The room fell silent and all eyes turned on him as he explained what had happened. He left out the part about Ivy purposely not taking the pill, but he did mention that she'd known he didn't want kids and that's why she never told him.

Antonio whistled and came back to the table. "I didn't know Ivy Johnson was the mother of your kid. Her family's got more money than—Derrick. They've been hitting the Forbes list for years. They're billionaires."

"Yeah, I know, but I had no idea who she was when I met her."

Antonio pointed at the beer on the table. "This lager is the most popular product in the line and the one that started it all. One of my female clients had an endorsement deal for them a few years ago when they launched a low calorie brew." Antonio was a publicist for professional athletes.

"How do you feel about this?" Matthew asked. He walked over and stood beside Antonio.

They were all looking at him with concerned eyes, as if he'd just announced that he had a life-ending disease.

He shrugged. "I'm good."

"Ivy's still letting you be a part of your daughter's life, right?" That was Roarke, the consummate family man.

"She is. I've been back to see her—Katie, I mean. We talk on the phone regularly, but to be honest, man, it's all so new." So new he felt overwhelmed, like someone had drawn a blanket of water over his head and he risked drowning. "I have a kid. I'm still not sure what I'm supposed to do with her." He chuckled and shook his head.

"You just be her dad," Roarke said.

"Hard to do from so far away," Matthew pointed out.

"But not impossible," Roarke insisted. "Celeste's ex lives somewhere up in that area, too, and he uses it as an excuse not to do anything for Arianna." Roarke was more of a father to his stepdaughter than her biological father ever was.

"I'm not going to be like him, that's for sure," Lucas said.

"How did your daughter react to finding out you were her father?" Derrick asked.

"Reserved. It was hard at first, but I found a way to connect with her and it helped a lot. We have a pretty good relationship now."

"Look," Roarke said thoughtfully. "It's a learning process, but it's one that you can manage. Just because you've never been a father doesn't mean you can't be a good one. Every man had to start somewhere."

"Easy for you to say. You've been doing it for years." Roarke had practically been groomed for fatherhood, since he'd raised his younger brother and sister from the time he was eighteen years old. "I'm nowhere near prepared."

"Well, at least you won't have to pay child support," Matthew said, with his usual attempt at humor. "That kid isn't going to need a damn thing from you."

"Don't listen to Matt," Antonio said. "Growing up, we had everything we could possibly want, but the best gifts were always the time we got to spend with my father when he wasn't traveling for a game. She's just getting to know you. That's what I'd concentrate on."

"How do you guys do it, though?" Lucas asked. He looked at Derrick and then at Roarke since they were the only ones who had children. "I only found out I was a father a few months ago, and already I want to lock her in an ivory tower."

Roarke laughed. "I don't think that feeling will ever go away. It's part of being a parent. It's hard, but we can't stifle them or hold them back from living their lives."

"Yeah, but it's probably different for you guys. Katie's all the way in Seattle. I'm not there to…I don't know, protect her."

"I understand what you're saying, but it doesn't matter if Violet's near or far, I'll always feel the same way," Derrick said. "I can't imagine a day when I won't want to protect her and her mother. Having them in my life creates a level of anxiety I never experienced before. I worry more about them than I do my own self. I want them to be fine, and I'll do whatever it takes to make that happen. I'd do anything for Violet and Eva. I would slay dragons for them."

The room fell silent as each man nodded. Lucas stared at the bottle of beer as he mulled Derrick's words. He looked up at a soft knock on the door.

"Come in," Derrick called.

His wife, Eva, looking very pregnant, appeared in the doorway holding their toddler, Violet, by the hand. The little girl wore footed pajamas with cartoon animals all over them.

"Hi fellas," Eva said.

There were *Hi Eva*'s all around.

Derrick rose from the chair with a frown on his face. "Sweetheart, what did I tell you about coming down those steep stairs in your condition? I don't want you hurting yourself or endangering my son."

"We are just fine." Eva emphasized the point by placing a hand on her protruding midsection. "Stop worrying."

"I'm having an intercom installed next week," he said.

"I told you no, this is your space and I don't need you to make it easier for me to reach you when you're down here."

Derrick didn't respond, and everyone in the room knew she'd already lost the argument even though he hadn't said a word.

"Fine," she said with a sigh. "I came down here because Violet's being fussy and wants her daddy to put her to bed."

"Night-night, Daddy." Violet stretched up her arms and Derrick lifted her up.

"You giving Mommy a hard time the way she does me?" he murmured.

"Don't tell her that," Eva said.

Violet wound her short arms around his neck and rested her head on his shoulder. She murmured something unintelligible and he kissed her on the forehead. "I'll be back in a few, guys. I'm going to put Violet down and get my hard-headed wife safely back upstairs."

"See how he treats me," Eva said to them, though she didn't look the least bit upset. The look on her face was more the contented look of a woman who knew, without a doubt, she was loved and adored. "Bye, guys." She waved and they all said good-bye to her.

Before the door completely closed behind them, Lucas could hear them fussing at each other as they climbed the stairs.

He twirled the bottle of beer on the table top. His friends had families to love and take care of. He'd seen the changes over the years as he got older. Friend after friend getting married. Some insisted they missed their bachelorhood, but others, like these guys, were different. They actually seemed happier with their wives. Even when they complained, he doubted they would want their lives any other way. They all belonged to a special club of husbands and fathers, and like pigs in slop, they were disgustingly fulfilled and content.

He'd steeled himself against wanting what they had, even insisted he was better off alone, but now a little part of him wanted this life. The craziness of chasing after a child, the annoyance of having a hard-headed wife who wouldn't listen, the stress of wanting the best for your family, and the need to love and be loved—unconditionally, even in the midst of screw-ups.

He swallowed against the tightness in his throat and gulped some of his beer.

He wanted all the good and the bad, the laughter, the tears—all of it—everything that came with finally having a family of his own.

As if conjured by his thoughts, the phone rang and the screen displayed Ivy's number. He answered right away.

"Hello. Umm…this is Katie."

Her soft, hesitant voice sent a tinge of worry to the back of his neck.

He stood and walked across the room for privacy and to get away from the robust conversation that had resumed between Antonio, Roarke, and Matthew.

"What's wrong, Katie?"

"I was wondering…"

In the background, he heard Ivy's voice. "Go ahead," she coached.

"Umm…I need a date for the father and daughter dance coming up at school, and I was wondering if…if you could come with me. It's short notice, and I know you're very far away, and if you can't, Uncle Cyrus said he'd take me."

He let out the breath he'd been holding and smiled in relief. For a minute he'd thought something serious had happened. "I can do that."

"You will?" Her voice contained elements of surprise and happiness.

"Of course I will. We're father and daughter, aren't we?"

"Yes," she said shyly, but the pleased sound of her voice suggested she was smiling.

"When is it?"

She told him which day in December the dance would take place. The date was oddly familiar, but he'd check his calendar once he ended the call with Katie. Before they hung up he assured her again that he would be there and she had nothing to worry about, and he meant it. As much as he could, he would be there—wherever and whenever she needed him—from here on out.

No other man was going to take his place again.

CHAPTER NINETEEN

The reason the date for the father and daughter dance had seemed so familiar was because it happened to take place the day before the wedding Lucas had promised to escort Priscilla to.

"We've been planning this for months." Priscilla stared at him in disbelief across the table. They sat in one of her favorite restaurants—an upscale soul food joint on the north side of town. He'd chosen it to soften the blow of canceling his plans with her. "You promised me you'd come." She couldn't comprehend how he could cancel on her, and he couldn't comprehend how she couldn't understand how important the dance was for him and his daughter.

"Katie needs me," he said, keeping his voice calm so he wouldn't set her off. "Right now, she's my priority."

"Attend the dance, and just come back the next day to make the wedding with me."

"If I go up there, I might as well stay for the weekend. I'm trying to get to know her."

Priscilla tossed the cloth napkin onto the tabletop. "Katie, or her mother?"

He leveled a stare at her across the table, noting how her lips had compressed into a thin line. "Don't start that again."

She seemed to think Katie wasn't the only reason he called Seattle. He couldn't deny hearing Ivy's voice was nice, but that wasn't why he called up there. Besides, ever since she'd overheard Priscilla talking to him, Ivy hadn't been as friendly. Polite, but not friendly.

"I can't avoid her mother."

"Of course not. But I can't help but wonder if the late night phone calls don't have something to do with your rich baby mama."

Lucas cringed. He really hated that phrase. "This isn't about Ivy. This is about me and you," he reminded her.

"I'm competing against Katie *and* Ivy."

"This isn't a competition."

"No?" Priscilla folded her arms across her chest. Despite her angry posture, he saw sadness in her eyes.

"No," Lucas insisted.

Her bottom lip quivered. "You don't even see me, do you?"

"Of course I see you. I know exactly who you are, darlin'."

"Don't darlin' me!" she snapped. "You *don't* see me." She swallowed. "This is going to be a regular thing, isn't it, where your family comes first?"

"My daughter," he corrected.

"You never even wanted children, and now all of a sudden you're running for father of the goddamn year," Priscilla said bitterly. The expletive surprised Lucas. She had to be very upset because she seldom cursed.

"Do you want me to pretend she doesn't exist? Would you respect a man like that—one who didn't take care of his responsibilities?"

She looked away for a few seconds before bringing her gaze to meet his again. "Should I respect a man who doesn't keep his word?"

Now she was really pissing him off, but he held his displeasure at bay. "I'll make it up to you."

"How? You're going to pay my rent again? Or maybe buy me a new car?"

"If that's what you want—"

"No, that's not what I want," she hissed, her eyes darting around to make sure no one in the restaurant overhead her. "How can you be so dense?"

Lucas calmly set his napkin on the table and searched for the right words. "Priscilla, I never—"

"I know. Don't you think I know that you never promised me anything? No marriage, no kids. You've made it very clear from the beginning." She'd accepted that he didn't want kids and had even said she could live without marriage, all to please him.

"That's not what I was about to say."

"Yet I'm still here, hanging out, waiting, wondering if you'll ever change. God, I'm an idiot." She sounded weary all of sudden.

"She's my daughter. I have eight years to make up for."

Priscilla laughed and took a huge swallow of her mint julep, draining the contents. She set the empty glass on the table. "Well, I guess eight years trumps five, right?" This was the most confrontational Priscilla had ever been. He'd never heard her use this tone of voice before.

"I'll make it up to you," Lucas said again.

"Yes, I know. You always do." A sad smile flitted across her face.

Lucas took a good look at Priscilla and wondered why she continued to put up with him. Why was it, no matter how many times they broke up, she kept coming back? And why couldn't he give her the permanent place in his life she so obviously wanted?

"Maybe we could go car shopping before you leave," Priscilla said. "I've had my eye on a Lexus hybrid. I think this time around I'd like to get a car that's a little better for the environment."

She signaled to the waiter and when he arrived at the table, she ordered another mint julep. The rest of the meal they discussed cars, and she gradually returned to her normal, non-confrontational self, as if nothing had happened.

But the tranquility didn't last.

Back at his condo, Lucas went into his home office to see if Brenda had left him a message about an upcoming project. Tension still existed between him and Priscilla, and he needed a break from pretending nothing was wrong. While he listened to a message from the freelance editor he worked with on his blog posts, a faint thumping sound came to him from somewhere in the condo. He went out to the living room in time to see Priscilla drop a suitcase at the front door.

"What are you doing?" he asked.

"I'm leaving. What does it look like?"

She went back into the bedroom and he followed. They'd been down this road before, but she'd never left him this soon after coming back. He stared as she dumped clothes and shoes into a black trash bag and slammed the dresser drawer shut. He hadn't even known she had enough stuff there to fill a suitcase and a large trash bag. Like she'd said at dinner, she was there, but he didn't really see her.

"I can't do this anymore," Priscilla said, scooping her lotions and

perfume off the dresser with a swipe of her hand. They la
bag on the floor. "Everything and everyone is always more imp
than me. One day you're traveling," she said, marching over to the
closet and yanking down a few dresses, pulling the hangers with
them. "Another time you've got an important event you can't
cancel."

Her comments rubbed him the wrong way. "My work is
important. You know that."

"Then your mother was sick," she continued, stuffing the dresses
into the same bag. She lifted her head, breathing heavily. "You never
put me first. Never."

She tied the top of the trash bag into a knot. "You need to decide
what you want. I'm giving you another chance, but I'm leaving you
and this time for good." She stood still long enough to shoot him a
look of defiance that still managed to look pleading. "Do you want to
be with me or not? I'm not getting any younger."

"'Cilla, listen to me—"

"Answer the question!"

Lucas fell silent. He didn't know what to say. He could give her
the answer she wanted to hear, but then he'd be a liar.

She shook her head in disgust. At herself, at him, he wasn't sure.
Her lower lip trembled and her eyes took on a shiny quality as they
filled with tears. "That's my answer, isn't it?"

She grabbed the trash bag and walked out to the living room. He
followed, still unable to find the right words. He made his living
using words, but right now he couldn't think of a single thing to say
to make the unfolding situation any less contentious.

"'Cilla, you don't have to leave. Stay and let's talk."

At the front door, she turned around. "My mother warned me.
She said after two years, a man knows whether or not he wants to
marry you, and if he's not talking about a future with you by then, it's
time to move on." Priscilla swiped a tear that spilled onto her cheek.
She sniffed. "She even told me I was foolish to stick around when
you made it clear you didn't want children, even though I do. And
when I told her you weren't interested in getting married, but I felt
pretty sure you would change your mind, she went ballistic. 'When a
man tells you the truth, believe him,' she said. And I still waited for
you to change your mind. But you haven't. Five years of my life is
enough, don't you think?"

She flung open the door and grabbed her suitcase. Instinctively he moved to assist her, but she swung around before stepping over the threshold. "In your book you said 'When a man wants you, make no mistake, he'll do whatever he can to hold onto you. He won't let you walk out that door, and if he does, trust he'll be right behind you.' You never once came after me, Lucas." Her voice cracked at the end.

This was obviously painful for her, but it was painful for him to watch, too, knowing he caused the hurt in her eyes. They'd been in a relationship for years based on his terms and his comfort level. He gave her material possessions, and in exchange she never pressured him for a commitment.

"Did you ever love me?" she asked. The question was one last plea, and he wanted to give her the answer she longed to hear, but he couldn't say the words if he didn't mean them, so he tried to find words that were the truth without deepening the embarrassment for her. Unfortunately, he took too long to respond. "Fuck you, Lucas. I hope you die a miserable, lonely old man," she said, and then she stormed out.

She struggled down the hallway with the suitcase and dragged the plastic bag behind her. He would have offered to help but knew his offer wouldn't be welcomed.

Lucas closed and locked the door. In a daze, he sank on to the sofa. He looked around at his place, his bachelor pad for years. A one-bedroom oasis from his crazy travel schedule and the women who came in and out of his life. He'd let Priscilla get closer than most, but was it because she was special, or because she kept coming back? With her, he'd never had to change, so he hadn't.

But she'd left him. The level of anger and pain in her face was different this time. She wasn't ever coming back again.

CHAPTER TWENTY

When Lucas arrived at Ivy's to pick up Katie for the dance, his daughter stared up at him with such elation in her eyes his heart swelled. He could get accustomed to that look, as if he was some kind of prize.

"How are you?" he asked, bending to give her a bear hug. She smelled like strawberries, probably from the pink lip gloss.

"I'm fine. Mommy hired a photographer to take pictures of us." She grabbed his hand and dragged him deeper into the condo.

Sure enough, Ivy and a photographer waited in the living room.

Ivy had made a big deal about the dance. In addition to sending their daughter to the hotel spa to get a mani-pedi with clear nail polish, she'd hired a stylist and hairdresser to get her ready. Katie's hair was styled in long ringlets, and her fuchsia headband matched the fuchsia dress she wore with its sparkling bodice and full skirt.

"Are you guys ready?" Ivy asked. "This is Katie's first date, so we have to take lots of photos."

"Wait a minute." Lucas removed the corsage from the box he'd brought in and attached the white petals to his daughter's narrow wrist.

"Pretty," Katie said.

Lucas straightened his black jacket and tie. "Now we're ready."

The photographer took photos of them standing next to each other and more with him crouched beside her, each with an arm around the other. Eventually they said their good-byes, and Lucas noted the wetness in Ivy's eyes but didn't comment.

He made a big production of opening doors for his daughter and made sure she was comfortable. He wanted to show her how she should be treated, so when she was older—much, much older—she'd already know what she deserved when some knuckleheaded boy stepped to her and wasn't about much.

Most of the attendees at the dance were parents or male figures, but a few mothers showed up, having escorted their daughters because a male family member wasn't available. If anyone thought it odd that Katie introduced him as her father, they never said, but their confused expressions spoke volumes. No one questioned him or his right to be there or even how she came to have another father.

His introduction made him realize that she still said father. Not "this is my dad" or "this is my daddy." Father sounded more detached to his ears, and he took that to mean he still had work to do. But he was willing to put in the time and effort.

He watched his daughter whisper and giggle with her friends, occasionally looking back to make sure he was still there. They danced to a variety of music and the professional photographer on hand took additional photos. His favorite was when he crouched beside the chair she sat in and she put her arms around his neck as if she would never let him go. She then gave him a big kiss, which the photographer manage to snap at the right moment.

The dance lasted a couple of hours, but as far as he was concerned, it ended too quickly. It was the most fun he'd had in a long time, which was strange. Who would have thought hanging out at a kid's dance would be considered a fun night out? He'd spent so much time drinking and bedding women over the years, he'd forgotten there were other equally satisfying ways to have a good time.

At the end of the night, they trickled out the doors with the rest of the attendees, and the driver pulled up to take them back to the condo. Katie, her stomach filled with punch, cake, and some amazingly good hors d'oeuvres Lucas couldn't believe they'd served to children, was fast asleep by the time they arrived at the hotel.

****

Lucas showed up with Katie in his arms, and after putting her to bed, Ivy returned to the living room to get a play by play of the evening. "How was it?" she asked.

"Excellent." He looked pretty happy. If she had to guess, he'd probably had as much fun as Katie. He whipped out an envelope of pictures and handed them to her. "These are your copies. I have mine." He patted his breast pocket. "I took more with my phone of her and her friends. I'll send those to you." He looked mighty pleased with himself. "So, what's the plan for tomorrow? I'm here for the entire weekend."

"If you like, you can spend the time with Katie. They don't have school tomorrow. You can take her to her play date in the morning, and tomorrow night she's all yours. Saturday I'm taking her over to my mother's house." Ivy flipped through the photos, smiling at the funny faces Katie and Lucas made at the camera. They looked like they had a blast. "I have plans with a friend, so I won't be here tomorrow night."

"You're going out?"

Ivy looked up at the note of surprise in his voice. "Yes. That's not a problem, is it?"

"No, not at all. I enjoy spending time with the little munchkin."

"And she loves spending time with you. So we're good?"

"Absolutely. So, play date tomorrow, and I'll bring her back afterward. That'll give me a chance to do a little running around. Then I'll be here before you head out."

He was in a really good mood, pumped up and energetic. All that smiling lit up his face and made him look so handsome. She swallowed past the lump in her throat and wished she didn't notice anything about him.

"Tomorrow night, then."

After he left, Ivy went back to her bedroom, contemplating their conversation. Their interactions were casual, but she still didn't know how to behave around him. They'd agreed to be friendly, for Katie's sake, but her attraction to Lucas hadn't dissipated one iota, and being around him still made her edgy. She felt the need to be cautious, steering around him like she had wet hands and he was electrified wire.

She was sitting up in bed, working on a report that needed to be turned in the next week, when a soft knock sounded on her bedroom door. The door cracked open and Katie came in.

"Hey, munchkin, what are you still doing up? I thought you were asleep."

"I was, but I woke up." She climbed into the bed and positioned her body the same as Ivy, laid back against the pillows with her ankle crossed over her knee. She stared up at the ceiling for a bit. "Mommy?"

"Mhmm." Ivy continued working on her laptop.

"I was thinking about something."

Ivy looked up from the report. "What's that?"

"I think I'm ready to call him daddy," she said quietly.

They'd talked about it once. Katie had loved Winston, and though she couldn't articulate her feelings, Ivy deduced she'd been worried about betraying him. She'd grown attached to Lucas and was torn. Ivy quickly allayed her fears, but her daughter had still held back.

"I think he'd like that very much," Ivy said.

A big grin spread across Katie's face. "Yeah. I think he'd like that, too."

CHAPTER TWENTY-ONE

Katie insisted on greeting Lucas at the door, and all Ivy could do was watch as she peered up at him. "Hi, Daddy."

Her voice lowered bashfully at the end and she stared down at her feet. She'd been too nervous to say it when he picked her up for the play date that morning, but she'd bolstered her nerves before his evening visit.

Lucas looked at Ivy, shock evident in his eyes. She held her breath and waited on his reaction. When his gaze landed on Katie again, it softened and a muscle in his jaw twitched.

"Hey, munchkin." His voice sounded hoarse.

Instead of giving her the customary hug, he lifted her into his arms and pressed his nose into her neck. He held her like that for a long time, standing in the doorway of the condo with Katie's arms wrapped tight around him.

Ivy's throat constricted and she blinked away tears. She'd dreamed about her daughter having a solid, healthy relationship with her father, and she was happy he hadn't held what she'd done against Katie and had embraced their relationship.

Lucas put down his daughter.

"You're ready to go?" he asked Ivy, his voice oddly husky.

"Yes, I guess I'll see you guys later."

They switched places. Ivy stepped outside the door and Lucas and Katie hovered on the threshold.

"Have fun on your date," Katie said. "We'll be fine."

"Date?" Lucas's eyes flicked to her, and he visibly stiffened. "With a man?"

"Uh...yes, actually." Why did she feel guilty all of a sudden, as if she'd done something wrong?

"Mr. Gil is taking Mommy on a date to the museum. Is he going to kiss you? Mwah, mwah."

"Katie, that's enough." That edgy feeling overcame her again, and with the weight of Lucas's stare on her, she felt distinctly uneasy. To Lucas, she said, "If you need me, I'll have my cell phone. It'll be on vibrate, so—"

"Got it," Katie and Lucas said at the same time.

Katie pinched her father. "Jinx."

"No, you're a jinx." He made to pinch her back, but she let out a high-pitched squeak and ran off.

"You better hide cause I'm coming to get you," he called after her. He turned back to Ivy. "Have a good time with your friend," he said, his tone derisive.

The change in attitude confused her a little. Why would he care that she was going out with a man when he had someone else in his life? She was the one living in the past, clutching onto memories.

She slipped her arms through the sleeves of her jacket. Coupled with a Chanel scarf doubled around her neck, the lightweight fabric was just heavy enough to keep her warm during the short walk to and from the museum.

"I'll be back in a few hours."

He had no reaction. She shot him another look, but his face revealed nothing, so she left, determined to have a good time.

****

"Would it be too presumptuous of me to ask you if I may come up?" Gil's eyes crinkled into a smile at the corners. Black and Pakistani, his exotic features had served him well in his younger days when he'd modeled.

Ivy wanted to want to have sex with Gil. It wasn't as if they hadn't many times before, but she couldn't muster the energy or desire as their evening wound down in the hotel lounge after they'd left the museum. They'd lingered over drinks while he made her laugh with his stories about his racially blended family in London and how they navigated the various holidays.

He then paid the tab and walked her to the bank of elevators. They stood off to the side, out of the way of others getting on and off.

"I have a daughter, Gil, you know that."

"And I'll never be allowed into the sanctuary of your condo so I can get to know her because I'm not the type of man you take seriously, am I right?"

They'd had this conversation before. Gil was a great lover, but he wanted to be serious. She preferred to keep the relationship casual, which meant he couldn't be introduced to her daughter as anything more than a friend. And he definitely couldn't spend the night.

"Gil…"

He tucked his hands into his pockets. "Not to worry, I won't give you a hard time, although I am curious about one thing."

"And that would be…?"

He studied her, weighing the question on his mind. "Why did you call me that night, a few months ago?" he asked.

"I told you, I changed my mind and wanted to go out."

"I asked you out when I saw you at the park, but you turned me down, and then all of a sudden you called and wanted to go out. I found that a bit odd."

"There's nothing odd about it."

He took a deep breath and stared at some point over her shoulder before he spoke again. "I care for you, Ivy. I've never made a secret of it. I understand that you don't want me to become a familiar fixture in your daughter's life—not unless we were serious, of course. It wouldn't do, and I respect your feelings on the matter. But I won't be used as a substitute for anyone. Do you understand?"

He'd seen through her feeble ruse to make herself feel better. "I didn't mean to—"

"I know, and I'm not upset, love. Matter of fact, I'm ridiculously happy that of all the blokes you thought of to fill this position, you chose me. But, I know how I feel about you, and I know how I want you to feel about me, and this won't work, you understand."

Ivy nodded. "I do." Remorse filled her.

He placed gentle hands on her arms. "You're a lovely woman, and any man would be lucky to have you. My regret is that I'm not that man. I understood the situation when your husband was alive, but I simply can't continue like this. I'm afraid I'm no longer willing to settle."

Their relationship had started years ago, and while he'd filled a void in her life, he wanted more than she could give. She'd been unfair—selfish even—to call him when she knew how he felt about her.

He pulled her into a hug and pressed his lips to her temple in a prolonged kiss, his embrace warm and solid. She held onto him a little longer than she should have, accepting this was probably the last time she would touch him. He'd held a very special place in her life for a long time. He'd helped her through some lonely nights when she'd needed affection and had no one else to turn to. She would miss him.

"Take care, love," he said. She watched him walk away and didn't move until she could no longer see him.

When she entered the condo, the first thing she noticed was the quiet and the shadowy dimness of the rooms. Only the light in the kitchen over the counters was on. Then she inhaled the familiar scent of chocolate and peanut butter in the air.

Lucas lay on the lounge chair near the window. She imagined he must have fallen asleep like that after a night of crossword puzzles and pizza—based on the empty box on the living room table. In the kitchen she found a couple of sandwiches left on a plate, the crust cut off the way she liked. They were filled with the strange but delicious combination of chocolate, peanut butter, and banana. Lucas had named the sandwich "the princess," after her.

She left the kitchen and peeked in on Katie before heading to her own bedroom where she tossed her jacket on the bed, removed her boots and tights, and slid her feet into a pair of comfy slippers. She shuffled quietly back out to the kitchen. Lucas was in the same spot, his eyes still closed.

She debated whether or not to wake him and then decided she'd eat one of the sandwiches first. As she picked one up, movement caught her eye. Her gaze collided with Lucas's and she smiled tentatively.

He eased off the furniture and stretched. His muscles rolled under the ribbed, long-sleeve T-shirt he wore. He looked completely at ease, and she tried not to think about the fact that he looked right at home there, as if he belonged. "I'll be right back," he said. Seconds later, she heard the bathroom door shut.

By the time he came out, Ivy had poured herself a glass of red wine in a long-stemmed glass and had already downed half of one of the sandwiches.

"You didn't waste any time," he said with mild amusement.

"Uh-uh." She had a mouthful of sandwich, so she couldn't say much.

"You're eating it cold?" he asked.

She swallowed. "Mhmm. It's good this way, too. Not as good, but good enough."

His gaze remained fixed on her, and she pretended not to notice, keeping her attention on the bread and then taking a sip of wine before setting the glass on the counter.

"How was your date?" he asked. She'd wondered if he would bring that up.

She paused in chewing, her senses on alert, and tried to figure out where the conversation was headed. She swallowed the last morsel. "I don't know if we should be discussing this." She stuck her thumb in her mouth and sucked off the remnants of chocolate.

"I'm just asking a question," Lucas said. "Being friendly, like you said we'd be. Nothing wrong with that."

She eyed him skeptically, still not sure where the conversation was headed and feeling a bit uneasy about it. "It was nice," she said cautiously.

"Why didn't you tell me you were going out with a man?"

"I guess I thought it would be weird."

"Nothing weird about that. We're adults, aren't we?"

"Yes, we are." Was he that indifferent to her? Was she the only one who felt the energy vibrating in the air between them?

"You have a good time with your friend at the museum?" he asked. He made the word 'friend' sound like a dirty word. His question didn't sound at all like an innocent inquiry, but she went along with the conversation.

"I did. We saw the Romare Bearden exhibit."

"I saw his work in Atlanta a couple of years ago. Did you like it?"

She relaxed into the conversation about the exhibit, a much safer topic. "Absolutely. Some of the collages were very striking. I even texted Cyrus. He's an art collector, and he's partial to African-American artists. He'd appreciate the work—assuming he doesn't already have Bearden pieces in his collection." She laughed. Knowing Cyrus, he probably did.

A muscle in his jaw moved. "You're in a good mood—smiling a

lot, so you must have had a good time."

"I did." On guard again, she kept her answer short on purpose. He was being pleasant enough, his tone neutral, but she couldn't shake the uneasiness. He seemed to be watching her closely.

"It must have gotten hot outside."

"Not in this weather." She frowned. "Why do you say that?"

"You left with your jacket on, but then came back with it off. Must have gotten hot." So he hadn't been asleep.

"I took it off once we came back into the hotel. I didn't need it anymore." She swallowed, feeling almost like she was under an inquisition.

"What did you do afterward?" he asked.

The line of questioning wasn't particularly intrusive. He was being quite casual about it, leaning against the counter and asking her about her date as if they really were two friends having a chat. Except they weren't just two friends.

"We went for a short walk. Then we had drinks downstairs and talked for about an hour or so."

"Planning to see him again?" This question wasn't asked in the same offhand tone. It was more deliberate, and his face had hardened.

"Probably not." Now would be a good time to cut him off. "But I don't think my relationship with Gil is any of your business."

"Actually, it is my business since you have him around my kid." He crossed his arms over his massive chest and his muscles bulged under the cotton.

"He's never been around Katie." Where had this come from?

"She knows who he is. She knows he gave you flowers on your birthday."

"Not that I owe you an explanation, but we were at Pike Place Market and ran into each other. I introduced him as a friend. We happened to be near a stand with organic flowers, and he bought a bunch for me because it was the weekend of my birthday."

Lucas continued his relentless grilling. "How well do you know this man?"

"Where is this going?"

"You have to be careful. We have a little girl."

He was back to that again. "Are you suggesting Gil would harm Katie? That's preposterous." She dismissed his comment with a flick of her hand.

"You can't be too careful."

"He's a good man."

"How would you know?"

She bristled, her back straightening. "I just do. I've known him for a long time—five years at least. He comes from a well-respected family. You're overreacting."

"I'll never overreact where Katie's concerned." His voice had become even harder.

Ivy backed up. "This is completely unnecessary. I know Gil very well, so I assure you, you have nothing to worry about."

"How well do you know him?"

"Well."

"You fucking him?" There was no mistaking the inflection now. Harsh, abrasive.

"Wh-what?" She wondered how the conversation had gone downhill in such a spectacular manner.

"I mean, while we're talking and being friendly, you can answer that, right? Friends can ask those kinds of questions and share information about what's going on in each other's love lives, can't they?"

"It's none of your business."

He came closer, his body tense, his eyes boring into her. "You planning on it? Fucking him, I mean."

She felt cornered and hot all of a sudden.

"You think you're just going to punk me," he continued, "got me sitting here babysitting while you run—"

"It's not babysitting, she's your daughter."

"—around with other men—"

"Now wait a damn minute, you and I don't have—"

"You think I'm going to let him come up in here and fuck you right under my nose? Like I'm some kind of chump? You think I'm going to allow that to happen again?"

She stared at him in disbelief. Again? What was he talking about? Anger flashed in the depths of his eyes. She'd never seen him so enraged.

"How can you even question me when you have a woman in Atlanta?" she demanded.

"She and I are done." He said it with such finality she was taken aback.

"When did that happen?"

"About a month ago."

"What about your other women?"

"There are no other women right now." His answer surprised her. She'd envisioned him with legions of women that he switched between according to preference when the need arose.

"So tell me," he said, his voice dropping a full octave, "you fucking him?"

He didn't deserve an answer, but since he'd told his relationship status, she gave him one. "We had something once but not anymore."

"Good," he ground out. "Because if I ever catch that pretty motherfucker up in here, I'll toss his ass out the goddamn window." He'd dropped his voice almost to a whisper, but that didn't negate the lethal threat in his statement.

Once again, his anger had come out of nowhere. But this time, she took a good look at him. It wasn't only anger that contorted his face. She saw pain, too.

CHAPTER TWENTY-TWO

Lucas had no right to question her. He knew it, she knew it.

Jealousy had blinded him and had turned him into someone he didn't recognize. He considered himself a lover, not a fighter, but his instinct where Katie and Ivy were concerned was to defend his...territory, for lack of a better word. Katie was his, and so was Ivy, whether she knew it or not. The minute he'd learned she had a date with Gil, he hadn't been able to think clearly.

The crossword puzzles had been a disaster. Because of his lack of concentration, they didn't finish a single one. He'd kept watch on the time, wondering where the hell Ivy and Gil were. The longer the night wore on, the more antsy he became.

Right now, he could only remember how she'd come in, smiling to herself, the jacket gone and wearing the sleeveless dress and scarf. Even her flawless makeup and the way the wine-colored lipstick shimmered on her lips bugged him.

It was one thing to think of her living the life of a single mother all alone. He'd even convinced himself he didn't care about her meaningless "friends with benefits" arrangements. But it was quite another thing have a face and name for the competition. To know she was developing a relationship with one man—dating, going to museums, having him buy her flowers. He tensed up at the thought that Gil had even gotten close enough to touch her. Meanwhile he had to dance around her and the livewire of attraction between them. It made him want to lock her up somewhere and keep the only key for himself so no other man could get near her.

"You know what, Lucas, you should go. You're obviously not thinking clearly." She marched around him, but he caught her by the arm and dragged her around to face him.

"Did you hear me?" he asked. If she didn't listen to him, he might lose his mind.

"I heard you. And now I want you to leave."

"I mean it, Ivy."

"What is it exactly that you want me to do? Live a celibate life forever so you don't get jealous? I have needs, you know."

She tried to twist away, but his hand tightened on the satiny skin of her arm. "I know all about your needs."

"I wasn't just talking about *those* needs. Sometimes I want to be held."

"You want to be held, I'll hold you. You want to be fucked, I'll fuck you. It's very simple. Let's not play games. We want the same thing."

"Really? Because I don't only want to be fucked, Lucas, I want marriage." Her eyes flashed at him, daring him to respond to that.

"You want to marry me?" A mocking smile slid across his face. "You sure about that? Because I don't have the pedigree. But your boy Gil, does, doesn't he?"

"Get out of my house right now. You've overstayed your welcome."

She tried to yank away her arm again, but he still wouldn't let go. Couldn't. They ended up in a staring match, both of them shooting daggers at each other.

His eyes narrowed on her. "You've known Gil for five years," he said slowly. "Did he fulfill your *needs* while your husband was still alive?"

This time she yanked harder and slipped from his grasp. He caught her around the waist in the hallway. "Let go."

He was up in her face now, searching her expression. "Answer me. Were you seeing Gil while you were married?"

"Let go, Lucas, I mean it. I told you to keep your hands off of me."

"*Tell me.*" He said it with urgency, desperation.

"Yes!" She vaulted the word at him with a vengeance.

Aghast, Lucas's mouth fell open. Even though he'd demanded a response, part of him had expected—or hoped for—a different answer.

"Are you satisfied?" Ivy asked. "Now you know the ugly truth. I'm a liar and you can add adulteress to my list of transgressions."

He stepped back in disgust, dropping his hands away as if her skin scalded him. "Were there any others?" he asked.

She averted her face.

"Son of a—" He laughed and shook his head in disbelief. "Poor sap. You cheated on Winston, got pregnant by me, and he forgave you. After all that, you still couldn't keep your damn legs closed long enough to give him the respect he deserved after accepting and raising another man's child? What the hell is wrong with you?" His question met with silence. "I got off easy," he said.

"Get out of my house, Lucas," Ivy said. "Your only concern should be for Katie. What I do in my private life is none of your business."

He closed in and braced a hand on either side of her. "You want marriage?" he asked. She flinched from the disgust dripping in his voice. "What man in his right mind would marry you when you don't understand the word commitment? But you're right about one thing, what you do in your private life is none of my business, darlin'. From now on, the only person I care about is Katie."

Only after he left did she let the first tear fall.

CHAPTER TWENTY-THREE

Lucas stared at the empty page on the computer screen. It was foolish of him to think that he could work after what happened at Ivy's, but he'd given it a try to avoid obsessing over her.

He scrubbed his hand down his face. He couldn't get their conversation out of his mind. Something wasn't making sense, and when something didn't make sense, he needed to understand why. From the look of it, Ivy had never been faithful to Winston. She'd started with him, Lucas, and continued with the same behavior even after she married him.

Maybe they'd had an open relationship. He'd done a series of blog posts on the topic, which had sparked a heated debate in the comments section of his blog. What he'd learned had been great material for his book. Maybe Ivy and Winston were into sharing.

No, that explanation still didn't make sense. He knew Ivy and couldn't imagine her in that type of a relationship. He didn't know squat about Winston Somerset, however.

He tapped the track pad and his computer screen came to life. He entered Winston's name into the search engine, but he couldn't find much on Ivy's husband. He came across a few photos here and there, including one of him with his father, a senator who'd had a surprise victory over his Democratic opponent years ago and was in the middle of campaigning for a second term.

Since doing his own research didn't help, Lucas picked up the phone and called Brenda. She'd been indispensable while working on his book, and she could get one of her people on this for him.

"Hello," she said in her usual chipper voice. She didn't have an off button.

"What are you doing up so late?" Lucas rose from the desk and went to settle on the sofa. He placed his feet on the low table in front of him and crossed his legs at the ankles.

"I had a premonition you'd call," she said.

"That's why I can't do without you. You anticipate my needs. I've got a project for you."

"What's up?"

"I need you to find out everything you can about Winston Somerset. S-o-m-e-r-s-e-t. He comes from a prominent political family in Seattle. His father is Senator Josiah Somerset."

"Looking for anything in particular?" she asked.

"No. Just whatever you can find."

"Budget?"

"None." Knowing more about Winston might help him understand Ivy better, and he didn't want cost to prohibit him from doing so.

"None?"

"That's what I said." He didn't elaborate, though she waited a few seconds for him to.

"What's your deadline?"

Having the information right away would be perfect, but he'd have to curb his impatience and be realistic.

"If you can get someone to work on it over the weekend, I'd appreciate it. I want everything you can find. Everything."

****

As it happened, Lucas didn't have to wait long. Either Brenda's researcher was a magician, or they were just that good. Either way, she called the next day with the research completed.

He was standing in the bathroom trimming his beard, and put her on speakerphone. "What do you have for me?"

"I put my best researcher on it. She didn't find much about Winston Somerset, but here are the highlights. He died two years ago and left behind a wife, Ivy Johnson, his high school sweetheart. They were married for seven years before he passed away. We found information about his charitable donations, but for the most part it seems he lived his life outside of the limelight and had no desire to enter into politics like his father. I'll clean this up and email it to you within an hour."

"Thanks for turning this around so fast."

"One more thing that was kind of unusual. We couldn't confirm Winston's death."

Lucas stopped in the middle of clipping his beard and frowned at the phone. "What do you mean? He is dead, isn't he?"

"Yes, he's definitely dead. It's just that we couldn't confirm *where* he died. There are conflicting reports. The first story has him dying in an apartment in Capitol Hill. The other has him collapsing in his car and found on the side of the road. The first story was, for lack of a better word, buried. We almost didn't find it. The one that's been officially reported is that he died in his car."

Had there been some kind of cover up in Winston's death? How was Ivy involved?

"Send me everything you have," Lucas said, "even if you don't think it's important."

"Will do."

****

With Katie at her mother's, Ivy took the opportunity to run errands. She'd dropped off her daughter earlier in the day to spend time at the house on Lake Washington. One of her mother's friends was visiting from Portland and had brought her granddaughter with her. Katie was there as a playmate for the other girl.

Ivy had just returned from an evening run to the store. Balancing a bag of groceries on her hip, she waited for the elevator doors to close. Instead of closing, a pair of large hands yanked them apart again. Lucas entered and filled the small space with his presence. She knew it wasn't a coincidence that he happened to be getting on the elevator at the same time. He must have been waiting around for her.

"We need to talk," he said.

"You said plenty last night. Unless you want to talk about Katie, we have nothing else to discuss."

"There's plenty for us to discuss. There's unfinished business between us, and there are things I need you to explain."

She had no idea what he was talking about. If he wanted to rehash their conversation from the night before, she wasn't interested. She should contact security and have him tossed out of the hotel, but she couldn't avoid him forever. They might as well have it out.

In the condo, he waited impatiently by the huge windows, tapping his foot every so often and looking in her direction. She knew because she kept track of him out of the corner of her eye while she unpacked the groceries. She took her time, completely uncaring that he had to wait. After the ugly accusations he'd thrown at her, she had no desire to accommodate him. When she finished she went into the living room and faced him, arms crossed, ready to do battle.

"You haven't been totally honest with me," Lucas said. Something was different about him tonight. He was still confrontational, but there was an air of decisiveness about him as well.

"I don't know what you're talking about."

"It doesn't make sense that less than two months after I left for Korea you ended up marrying another man. How could you be high school sweethearts and engaged when you spent the entire summer making love with me?"

He considered what they'd done making love. She tried not to read too much into it. For her it had been making love, but because he'd left so easily, she'd assumed that for him their times together had simply been sex.

"I met you, and I wanted you," Ivy said, keeping her voice cool.

"Just like that?"

Ivy shrugged.

"Okay, fine." He stroked his chin. "Maybe I'll accept what you say. How did your husband die?"

Ivy stiffened. "What does his death have to do with anything?"

"How did he die? Brain aneurysm, right?"

"Yes, I told you that before."

"Where did he die?" He threw the questions at her as if he was trying to get her off balance.

"They found him on the side of the road—"

"You're lying."

"What are you getting at?"

"I'm getting at the fact that I had someone look into your husband's death and she found two different stories. One story was buried so deep she almost didn't find it."

Her eyes widened. "You did what?"

"Because of all the half-truths. I didn't have a choice. So don't play the holier-than-thou card with me. Answer the question."

"What difference does it make?"

"Because I want to know the truth once and for all. The truth about everything. The truth about you, and me, and Winston. What the hell happened? What kind of marriage did you have that you would sleep around on him even after you married him? That he would accept my daughter as his own, even though you were childhood sweethearts and supposedly secretly engaged? None of this makes any sense!"

"Why is it important to you what I did after you were gone?" Ivy demanded. "You left, because we weren't—" Unexpectedly, pain arrowed through her. "We weren't a forever thing. Your words. You didn't care about my feelings. You told me to move on and said I'd get over you. Do remember saying that?" A torrent of words gushed from her.

"And you did, is that what you're telling me?"

They were both yelling now.

"It was impossible. How could I forget about you when I was carrying Katie? But you managed to forget about me quite well. You just turned off your emotions like that summer never even happened." Her life had been changed, his had gone on as usual.

"That is not what happened, Ivy."

"No? That's exactly what happened from my point of view."

She'd been convinced she could change him. Love him more, love him harder. But in the end, it had all been a wasted effort. He'd left her anyway and told her to forget about him, but she'd never been able to. No matter how hard she tried.

"Don't talk about things you don't know anything about," he ground out.

"The poems were fake, your feelings were fake."

He came at her. "My feelings were real. I damn near worshipped the ground you walked on."

"You just left, Lucas!" She flailed her arms. She wouldn't cry. She couldn't, but it was so hard not to when the memory of his departure returned as an avalanche of anguish. "You ran halfway around the world—"

"I told you from the beginning I had plans to leave—"

"You left, without a backward glance. Didn't I mean *anything* to you? You ripped out my heart and forgot all about me."

"*I came back for you!*"

The pain in his face, the agony in his voice was unmistakable. His hands closed into two meaty fists as he fought against the emotional turbulence. "I came back for you, Ivy. Never. Not once did I forget about you in the past nine years. Don't think I didn't try."

Ivy stared at him in stunned silence. She shook her head in denial. "You couldn't have come back," she whispered. "When?"

He walked away and stared out the window. He didn't speak for a long time. He seemed to be gathering his strength, forcing himself to calm down. "I got all the way over there," he said, "and one month in I couldn't do it. I realized I'd made a mistake, but I'd signed a contract, and I had to fulfill my obligations." She could only see his profile, but his Adam's apple bobbed as he swallowed. "I finally convinced them to let me leave. I left my post in South Korea and made arrangements to come back as soon as possible." When he spoke again, his voice was heavier, his tone harsher.

"I wanted to surprise you, but I came back and Mama Katherine showed me the article. Ivy Johnson, daughter of Cyrus and Constance Johnson of Johnson Enterprises. Married to her high school sweetheart." A short, bitter laugh left his lips. "I didn't believe it. I thought it was some stupid, made up story. I hoped it was, anyway. But it wasn't. It was very real." He turned to face her. "Don't tell me about forgetting. I was gone—what…five, six weeks at the most? And you were already married to Mr. Pedigree. Mr. Everything-I-wasn't. I wanted to fight for you, I wanted to tell him to go fuck himself because you were mine, but who the hell was I? Nobody. And you'd made your choice."

That's how he'd known about her marriage. He hadn't been in South Korea. He'd been home, on U.S. soil.

"Lucas—"

"What could I give you?"

"What do you mean? I don't want—"

"I have nothing." He clenched his jaw to restrain himself. She could see the internal struggle in his face, in his posture. "You have everything. All this wealth, your family—you can trace your roots back for generations on both sides of your family. I left because you deserved better. You didn't understand what you were getting with me. Nothing."

"Don't say that."

"It's true," he said, his voice harsh. "I don't know my medical history. I don't know who I am. Does diabetes run in my family? Do I have siblings? I may never know."

She hurt for him. To think, he thought he wasn't good enough because he didn't know his background. He thought he couldn't compare to Winston and what his family offered.

"Lucas..."

"I listened to your stories about growing up with your brothers and your parents and your summers at Camp Atwater in Massachusetts, the Jack and Jill activities your parents made you attend so you could meet the right boys from other blue blood families."

"I was just talking, complaining, sharing my life with you. I never thought it would make you jealous or feel insecure."

"I wasn't jealous. I wasn't insecure. When you told me those stories I became curious. I've always been curious about other people's lives because my life was so shiftless for the first fourteen years. I went from home to home, and I made damn sure I acted out so they would want to get rid of me because I didn't want to need them. Mama Katherine was the only person who never gave up on me. I don't know where I'd be if it wasn't for her—if she hadn't handed me a pencil and paper and said, 'If you get angry, write it down. Put your thoughts on paper instead of running all over hell and halfa Georgia acting like a damn fool.'" That sounded like something she would say. He smiled a little at the memory. She didn't think he could help smiling whenever he talked about his mother. "She straightened me out, but that's my story. It's nothing like yours. What can I possibly offer you?"

Ivy looked deeply into his eyes. "I never wanted anything from you. I just wanted you. I loved you, Lucas, and eventually I told myself I didn't anymore. I had to, so I wouldn't go crazy, looking into Katie's eyes, so much like yours. Every day. *Every day.*"

"If you loved me so much, how could you marry another man so soon after we broke up? Were you really secretly engaged to him?"

"No, I wasn't engaged to him," Ivy said quietly.

"You weren't?"

"I-I didn't know that you would come back. If..." If she'd known. If she'd only known, she wouldn't have married Winston. She wouldn't have succumbed to the despair of thinking she'd lost Lucas for good.

"I don't know if that makes it any better," Lucas said. "From where I'm standing, that summer meant a helluva lot less to you than it did to me. When I found out you were married, I begged; I groveled to get my job back. I spent three years over there. I signed up for two extra years so I wouldn't have to come back to the States."

"I wouldn't have married him if I'd known how you felt. If I'd known you were coming back."

"Why? Didn't you love him?"

"I did." She still missed him sometimes. He'd been the perfect companion. "When Winston died, I was devastated. He was my best friend, but…we didn't have a normal marriage. I loved him but I wasn't *in* love with him."

Lucas's brows drew together into a deep vee. "What are you saying?"

"Winston and I were helping each other out. We had a marriage of convenience. My husband was gay."

Chapter Twenty-four

Ivy told him the whole story from the beginning, filling in the blanks and responding to the invisible question marks in his research.

After confirming her pregnancy, and with Lucas gone and having made it clear he did not—under any circumstances—want to be a father, she'd married Winston out of necessity. He'd been the one to suggest it after she'd confided in him, and they'd orchestrated a self-imposed shotgun wedding.

She already had a reputation because of the sex tape and had run to the eastern part of the country to go to college and escape the knowing looks from the high society mavens and the occasional leer from her father's business associates. For the most part she'd managed to fly under the radar in Atlanta. But getting pregnant with no father in sight would only revive the rumors, and the last thing she wanted to do was end up in the papers again.

For his part, Winston felt wholly responsible for his father's defeat in the last senatorial race. Winston's sexuality had come into question by "unnamed sources." His father had run on a conservative platform, touting family values, which had been lambasted by his opponents through innuendo. Even perfectly innocent photos of Winston in the company of other men managed to raise eyebrows.

A long time passed before they confessed the truth about Katie's parentage. By then, Ivy's father had been dead nearly two years, and the Somersets were so in love with Katie they considered her their grandchild anyway. The fact that she wasn't blood meant nothing to them.

Since Ivy and Winston didn't have a real marriage, they had an understanding. They lived together in a mansion outside of Seattle, but she had her lovers, and he had his. Eventually Winston settled down with one man, but discretion was key. He rented an apartment in his boyfriend's name in the Capitol Hill neighborhood, known for its nightlife and gay population. He and his boyfriend met there regularly.

Ivy also settled down with one person, in a more casual relationship than Winston had with his lover. Her relationship was built on trust, and because she simply liked Gil best. Initially they had their clandestine hookups in posh hotels, but when they started seeing each other more regularly, it made more sense for them to have a place of their own. She rented a pied-à-terre inside the city limits where they could meet when he was in the country.

There was the occasional rumor about their marriage being a sham, but without concrete evidence, they always fizzled out.

Winston's death had been completely unexpected. He'd complained of a terrible headache early in the evening, and though he was due back at the mansion, he'd told her he would remain at the apartment in Capitol Hill. His boyfriend had called her with the devastating news. She, with help from Cyrus, paid off the right people to keep the story quiet and released a counter story to protect Winston's reputation and the lie they'd been living all along.

Lucas hadn't said a word the entire time Ivy had been talking. He let her get it all out, and she felt spent after the confession.

"If I'd known you'd come back, I would have never done any of it." She felt compelled to tell him again.

"Why did you get pregnant against my wishes?" he asked.

She couldn't tell if he was angry. He hardly moved, and it was difficult to see his face clearly with his back to the window.

"I was wrong. I know I was wrong."

"Why did you do it?" he asked.

"You told me you didn't want a child. I don't blame you for being upset."

"Why?" he prodded. He inched closer, peering at her with dark eyes that seemed to want to look into her soul.

Ivy twisted her grandmother's turquoise ring on her finger. "Because I was desperate to hold onto a piece of you," she admitted in a low voice. "I know it was selfish, but I didn't just want a baby. I wanted *your* baby. I—"

She never finished her little speech.

Lucas pulled her roughly into an embrace that had their lips crashing together. The way his mouth landed on hers, it was as if he'd been waiting for this moment, for that specific confession. For her part, Ivy became a ravenous being and immediately dived into the kiss, her arms crossing behind his neck to pull him closer. It went on for an eternity, becoming more aggressive as passion overtook them.

Her tongue swooped into his mouth and her senses recognized him—his taste, the way he smelled, the way the short hairs felt under her palm as she caressed the back of his head. He kneaded her breasts and turned the nipples taut, transforming them into aching peaks that protruded from her blouse. She shuddered with reaction and wriggled against him, straining to get closer—to do anything to assuage the feverish need that now heated her loins.

No more words were needed and no need to atone for actions from the past. All that was left was a burning desire to strip naked and feel his skin against her skin.

They stumbled toward the bedroom, bouncing against the walls of the hall and clumsily tearing at each other's clothes. They couldn't get out of them fast enough. His shirt was yanked over his head and her panties discarded with a flick of her foot. Shoes, bra, trousers—all were tossed aside and left a trail to her bedroom door.

They burst into the semi-dark room and toppled on to the bed. On the mattress they rolled once, twice, until she lay sprawled beneath his muscular frame. This position she knew well and had longed for too many times to count.

His hand curled between her legs to find her hot and wet; her body jerked and she gasped at the impact. She almost couldn't breathe from the abundance of pleasure the slight touch evoked. His fingers explored the fine hairs and gently kneaded the swollen flesh, and when he slipped the middle digit between the folds, an urgent moan spilled from the depths of her throat.

She raked her tongue across his Adam's apple and dragged her teeth lightly against his earlobe. His ears were sensitive, and she felt the tremor that coursed through him. He rolled over, pulled her on top of him, and then he grabbed her butt to grind his erection into the moist cleft between her legs.

"Lucas," she breathed, running her hands over his beautiful, dark skin.

It was almost unreal to think that she had him in her bed. Her fingers skated over the curly hairs sprinkled on his chest and traveled to the ridged muscles of his abdomen. Big and hard, he was the perfect male specimen; his body contained all the ingredients for unforgettable lovemaking—muscular arms, thick, powerful thighs, a strong back, and one long, steely erection to drive away coherent thought and the memory of any other man.

Ivy dipped one breast into Lucas's mouth, and he lapped at the tip, groaning in frustration when she withdrew. She did it again, but her teasing came to a halt when he caught her by the waist and pushed her onto her back. Holding her hands pinned above her head, he took his time and licked his way across her chest, from one breast to the other. He savored each one, plucking the walnut-colored peaks between his thick lips and sending shockwaves to her clit.

The moist swirl of his tongue and the rough texture of his beard across her sensitive skin ignited her nerve endings. She arched her back and opened her legs wider, letting him simulate sex with a slow grind. The pleasure was almost too much. She tossed her head from side to side, confined to one position because he held her captive so he could feast on her breasts without restriction. He was relentless, sucking her swollen nipples, licking at the curved mounds, burying his face in the valley between them.

Just when she thought she couldn't possibly take anymore of the delicious attack, without notice, he turned her onto her stomach.

"This is what I want right here," he said.

His hand palmed her butt in a display of possession, and she tilted her hips higher, wantonly rubbing her bottom against his crotch.

"Can't wait, can you?" he asked in a rough voice.

His hand landed with a loud smack on her bottom. Ivy cried out and bowed her back into a deeper curve. Feverish warmth expanded from the point of impact and sent an erotic wave through her body.

"Don't you ever lose this ass," he said. His voice sounded dark and thick.

He hit her again, and the stinging blow sent a rush of heat to her wet core. Teetering on her hands and knees from the onslaught, she closed her eyes to relish the pain.

"More," she whimpered, pushing back against him.

He sucked air between his teeth and obliged her demand, hitting her again and again. Every time he did the blow made her buttocks jiggle and sent an echoing pulse to her clit. She fell onto her elbows, mouth agape, gasping and weak with pleasure.

"Look," Lucas said.

Ivy twisted her head and saw what he saw, the two of them reflected in the window—she on her elbows and knees and he behind her.

He sat back on his haunches and lifted her knees onto his thick thighs. The position made it easy for him to kiss the bruised flesh of her butt cheeks, prompting a different kind of sensation. He soothed her with delicate kisses and moist licks of his tongue. A touch that was softer, more tender in pressure.

"I love the way you smell," he breathed, yanking her higher.

Then he pressed his mouth to her sex. Ivy cried out, but he tightened his hold, keeping her in a vulnerable position that had her backwards and almost upside down in front of him.

"Goddamn, you taste so good," he panted. He tilted his head and licked her damp flesh as if he couldn't get enough. It was a complete and thorough ravishing that left her tearing at the sheets, breathless with her head spinning.

A sound came from him, half groan, half growl. His mouth continued its merciless assault on her body, and like a voyeur, she couldn't tear her eyes away from the sight of his face pressed between her legs, mirrored in the glass. The erotic image propelled her to the edge at a faster pace, and when she climaxed, her entire body shook from the force of it.

Lucas eased her on to the bed on her stomach and trailed soothing kisses up her back. It felt as if he covered every inch of skin. She luxuriated in the attention, purring and stretching like a satisfied cat.

"We're not done yet, darlin'."

She hoped not, because she still hadn't felt *him* inside of her. And she wanted that, more than anything.

He rolled her over and fixed two pillows beneath her hips. He covered her body with his, and she closed her arms around his warm, solid torso. She stroked the satiny muscles and ran her hands down his back to his firm posterior. She urged him forward, and with one stroke he burrowed to the hilt.

Her head snapped back and she whimpered as her body came

alive again. Only he could do this—turn her into a livewire so quickly, so thoroughly. She pressed her feet into the mattress to meet each downward stroke. Rolling her hips, she matched his tempo, and her pliant body twisted unrestrictedly beneath him.

"*Goddamn*, Ivy, wait a…" His voice trailed off when she tightened her muscles. He swore viciously, his rhythm stumbling.

She felt powerful in that moment, as if she was in control.

"You got the good shit," he said. His voice was tight, as if he barely got the words out. "This my shit now," he said, stroking harder, delving deeper. His eyes met hers in the glass. "Let me hear you say it. Let me hear you say this is mine."

Her muscles clenched around him as she neared another orgasm. "Yours, Lucas. This is your shit."

"Damn right."

Her arms tightened around his shoulders and her ankles folded at the base of his spine. In the glass, their brown bodies locked together so tight it was hard to tell where one ended and the other began.

"All mine."

"Yes. All yours."

He swelled inside of her and she sensed how he struggled to hold back.

"Don't stop," she begged. She was so close. "Please. Not yet."

"I'm not gonna last much longer," he grunted.

His arms flexed and his throat drew taut as he wrestled with self-control. Clenching his teeth, he increased the speed of his thrusts, turning the sweet ride into a chaotic inferno of heat in her pelvis.

It was just what she needed. Pressure tugged in her stomach and she exploded around him. Tears sprang to her eyes as her body shuddered through a climax that battered her senses and tightened her spine.

"I love you," she cried out as wave after wave of pleasure doused her body in flames.

"Say it again," Lucas commanded, pumping faster.

"I love you. I love you." Her hips moved spasmodically in time to the words as she rode out the orgasm.

With a hoarse, pained sound, Lucas buried his face in her neck and came. His big body shook and he grabbed at her hips, grinding his pelvis between her thighs.

"Ivy," he gasped in a husky voice. His body trembled above her.

After a long time, he finally caught his breath and lifted his eyes to hers. "I love you, too."

CHAPTER TWENTY-FIVE

Ivy stretched and slid her leg between Lucas's thighs. The hairs there tickled her skin and underlined the contrast of his masculine body to her feminine form. He lay on his back with his eyes closed and she was half on top of him, drained of energy but very content.

His eyelashes brushed his cheekbone, and she couldn't resist swiping a finger over the curled hairs.

"Watch it," he warned. "You'll poke my eye out."

"It's so unfair," she said.

He grunted.

She touched his beard, letting the bristles abrade her fingertips.

"What do you think?" he asked.

"I like the beard," she said.

He twisted his head on the pillow to look at her. "So I can keep it?"

"Yes, you can." She rested her head on his shoulder and smiled into his neck.

"How about a shower?" He ran a hand in a leisurely stroke over her hip and thigh, applying a pleasurable warmth to her skin everywhere he touched.

Ivy moaned and rolled away from him. "I'm too lazy."

"Come on." He smacked her bare bottom.

"Stop." She rubbed her flesh and watched him climb out of bed. She bit her knuckles to keep from screaming in delight as she watched the corded muscles of his shoulders and back ripple under the dimmed overhead lights.

"Quit looking at my ass," he said, heading toward the adjoining bathroom. "I'm not a piece of meat."

"I'm not looking at your flat ass."

"Ha, nice try," he hollered from the bathroom. "I get a lot of compliments on my ass, thank you very much." He deserved those compliments. He had a beautiful behind, firm and taut like the rest of him. She loved grabbing it as encouragement to sink deeper into her body.

She sat up and yelled, "And apparently all those compliments have gone to your head." She flopped against the pillows in a fit of giggles, feeling very pleased with herself.

"What the hell are all these gadgets?"

Ivy sat up again. "It's a steam shower. It doubles as a sauna," she explained.

No sound came from the bathroom for a while, then, "Is this a radio?"

She laughed at the incredulous tone of his voice. "It's a control panel, but yes, there's a built-in radio, too."

"Bet you haven't used any of this, have you?"

"Yes, I have." In all honesty, she'd only taken advantage of the sauna once, right after she moved in. She hadn't used it since.

"You coming in here to help me with all these buttons, hoses, and other contraptions? I just want to take a shower."

Ivy groaned dramatically so he could hear, but she scooted off the bed and entered the bathroom to find him standing outside the glass enclosure. As soon as she was close enough, he grabbed her and dragged her into the shower with him and closed the door. Which had probably been his plan all along.

"My hair!" she shrieked. She lifted her hands to her head, but he ignored her protests and turned on the water, drenching them both in the warm pellets gushing from the overhead fixture and the body jets.

"I'm going to get you," she said, thumping his hard chest.

"Don't hurt yourself," he said with a cocky grin. Then he dipped his head and captured her mouth.

They made love in a rush, devouring each other as if it was the last chance they'd ever have. Tongue, teeth, lips traveled over soaking wet skin. Lucas lifted her against the wall and thrust upward, his hard flesh pulsing inside the snug fit of her body. They slammed together, grinding, pumping, until the tempo increased.

"You feel so good," she whimpered. "Don't stop, don't stop." Her breathless chants had him pounding harder, pushing deeper until their orgasms erupted at the same time.

They shuddered through the climax, clinging tight and panting heavily. Her fingernails dug into his shoulders, and he gripped her so hard she had no doubt he'd leave handprints on her ass. Eventually, normal breathing took the place of the shallow pants, but they remained bound together for a while as water rained down on them.

****

"Do you still write poetry?" Ivy asked.

She looked relaxed, having changed and teamed a pair of designer jeans with a white fitted T-shirt. Her damp hair was wrapped in a towel while she prepared omelets for them as a late dinner. Lucas followed her instructions for the preparation of salad dressing using red wine vinegar and Dijon mustard.

"Nah."

"Why not?"

The noise of the blender filled the kitchen. When he turned it off, he answered. "Because they were so corny."

"I liked them." She sounded defensive, as if he'd insulted her poetry. She slid the last omelet onto the plate.

"I wasn't any good," he said. "I haven't written anything in years."

Not since they split. Before he'd met her, he'd written poems, but they'd been mostly about societal problems. After meeting Ivy, most of what he wrote had become love poems. She'd been his muse, and he hadn't written anything after they broke up.

"Do you remember any of them?" She looked at him expectantly.

"Hardly."

"None?"

"Nah."

"They were nice." She poured dressing into a bottle. "You want to know which one I really liked?"

"Which one?"

"The Sun and the Moon," she responded, a wistful note in her voice.

Lucas groaned. "One of the worst ones." He remembered it. He'd spit out the words one night as they walked back to his apartment.

"It wasn't so bad," she said quietly. "'You're beautiful, boo. The sun and the moon ain't got nothing on you.' Do you remember the rest?"

"A little bit." He'd been inspired by her beauty that night, feeling romantic, walking hand in hand after a night of spoken word at a nearby café. This woman, who could have any man she wanted, had wanted him. The poem had started as a silly rhyme, but soon he realized it accurately summed up his feelings for her.

She looked up from the meal preparations, and he recited the words. "The stars in the sky can't match the stars in your eyes. The prettiest gem in the world cannot compare to you. If asked, I would say, that's the God's honest truth. Anyone who says different, I would call them a fool. Cause the sun and the moon ain't got nothing on you."

She stared down at the plate in her hand.

"Ivy?"

"I wish..." There was a breathless, pained quality to her voice.

He took the plate from her and set it on the counter. He pulled her into his arms. Her soft body molded to his, and she smelled like the lilac lotion he'd rubbed into her skin after their shower.

"No regrets," he said. "We both needed to grow up, I think."

She laid her head on his chest and wrapped both arms around his waist. "It doesn't stop me from wishing things had been different."

****

They ate their meal in front of the television and afterward Ivy sat on the couch, snuggled beside Lucas. She still had her hair wrapped in a towel.

"What do you want to do tonight?" she asked. Tomorrow she had to pick up Katie from her mother's house, and he flew back to Atlanta the next day.

"Why? You have something in mind?"

"Maybe." She peeked up at him.

"What?" he asked in a guarded voice.

"I think you should try your hand at spoken word again."

He groaned and let his head fall back against the sofa. "Come on, Ivy."

She disentangled herself from his arm. "Why not? You're talented."

"It's a waste of time."

"Why?"

He shrugged. "There's no money in it, for one. And I...I don't have any interest."

"I can't believe that. When you recited your poetry, it always turned me on," she said.

He raised a brow. "Oh, yeah?"

"Yes." She leaned in. "Do you think you could still do it?" she asked, a coaxing, seductive tone to her voice.

His gaze became speculative. "I could try, but…"

"You should try. Recite some of the old lines or try something new. Come on. I know just the place." She jumped up from the couch.

"Wait a minute, I didn't say—"

She ignored his protests, hurrying toward the rear of the condo. "Let me blow dry my hair and then I'll be ready."

Less than an hour later they sat in Ivy's car in the parking lot of The Underground. She'd pulled her hair back into a sleek ponytail. To her ensemble she'd added a tailored jacket and Tacori diamond-surrounded amethyst earrings with the matching bracelets. Lucas had paired his jeans with a long-sleeved white shirt that highlighted the rich brown color of his skin.

"What is this place?" Lucas asked.

"It's an underground club—hence the name. It's not popular enough to be mainstream, but it has a loyal customer base. They offer good exposure for local bands. Mostly indie rock and socially-conscious hip-hop. Each night there's a different theme. Trent's frat brother owns it."

"Looks like a place for twenty-somethings. I'm too old to be hanging out with these young kids."

Ivy laughed. "It's for us older folks, too. Trust me, everyone is welcome. Trent's band plays here every so often, but tonight is spoken word." The end of the last sentence ended on a hopeful upswing.

"I don't know if I can do this, Ivy. It's been a long time."

"You can be anyone you want to be here. No one cares," Ivy said.

"I'm an old thirty-something. I don't do that kind of thing anymore."

"Are you saying you no longer have it in you?"

"Maybe."

She fell quiet. Disappointed, but not wanting him to participate if he had no interest, Ivy sighed heavily. "Let's go then."

"Wait a minute." Lucas placed his hand on the steering wheel to stop her. He sat for a minute, the light from the neon sign illuminating his face in the dark car. "Okay, let's do it."

"Yay!" She clapped rapidly.

He grinned at her. "Now I see where Katie gets that clapping thing she does."

"I only do it when I'm excited."

"I see. Come on before I change my mind."

They walked up to the front door hand in hand, reminiscent of the times they'd done the same that summer in Atlanta. Inside, Lucas added his name to the list of spoken word performers. After he finished, Ivy texted her brother Trent, who was there with his best friend. He texted back and they found them at a well-placed table in the middle of the club with an excellent view of the stage.

A young woman wearing glasses and her hair pulled back in what looked, from Lucas's vantage point, to be a bun, sat next to Trenton.

"This is Alannah," Trenton said, by way of introduction.

Alannah was a cute girl, but not the kind of woman Lucas expected Trenton would hang out with. Not that he knew Trenton well at all, but they didn't strike him as the kind of people who would naturally gravitate to each other. She'd probably draw more attention to herself if she styled her hair in a different way and dressed more appropriately for her size. Her jacket practically swallowed her body, as if she was hiding under it.

She almost seemed to want to disappear into the background, despite the fact that Trenton had his arm draped on the back of her chair. Over the course of the evening, a few women approached him, and when they did, Alannah stared more steadily at the stage. At one point, she excused herself from the table and a waitress came over. Trenton ordered her a Coke and lime.

"You don't think she'll want a real drink?" Lucas asked.

"She always has two drinks tops. She can barely manage that. Then she drinks Coke with lime for the rest of the night."

"You know her well," Lucas observed.

"They know each other well," Ivy chimed in. "They've been best friends for about twenty years. They're like an old married couple."

"She's practically my sister," Trenton said. "Gotta protect her from the riff raff. I look out for both of my sisters." He looked pointedly at Lucas. "Chase off the bad ones." He definitely wasn't subtle.

"You're not happy with me, I take it?" Lucas asked.

"I'm a little skeptical about your intentions." He glanced at his sister, who gave him a look that clearly said *Shut up*. He ignored her.

"You don't have to worry about me," Lucas reassured him.

"You're right, I don't, as long as Ivy and Katie are happy. Anything less than happy, we have a problem."

Lucas appreciated Trenton's forthrightness. In fact, based on everything he'd seen so far, Ivy and Katie didn't lack positive male figures in their lives. He counted that as a plus.

About twenty minutes later, the MC called Lucas's name. He rose slowly from the chair and Ivy grasped his hand in hers. He looked down at her. "Knock 'em dead," she said.

"I intend to."

Lucas considered his workshops and panels around the country a kind of performance, so he wasn't nervous about being in the spotlight. He loved the rush of excitement he felt in front of an audience.

But this was a different type of performance, and much more personal.

After getting up on stage, he gripped the mic in one hand and leaned over it, bringing his mouth so close to the instrument his lips almost touched its shiny, silver surface. He lowered his voice to a warm bass. "Hello, my name is Lucas. I'd like to dedicate this poem to my princess. No, my queen. It's simply called, *I Can't Sleep*."

"Woohoo!" Cheers and claps encouraged him.

"Bring it on, baby!" someone yelled.

The lights lowered and a spotlight trained on him, casting the audience into shadowy obscurity. His eyes met Ivy's and he felt the old Lucas coming back. She gave him the thumbs up sign and a smile of encouragement.

Completely unrehearsed, the words and poetic cadence came to him. Extemporaneous and inspired by the woman he'd never stopped loving. He lowered his voice even more before he let the words flow past his lips.

I can't sleep
And it's your fault.
I think about you night and day.

I absolutely love the way
Your laughter cheers me when I'm down,
The way your smile spreads sunshine all around,
To everyone, anyone,
Lucky enough to be in your presence,
To bask in your light.
I can't sleep.
Because I'm watching as *you* sleep,
Curled in my arms
Your soft skin brushing mine,
Your hair trailing across my chest
Spreading sensation, elation, and satiation to my dark,
Empty soul.
I can't sleep.
I know how lucky I am. And if I close my eyes,
I might wake up and realize,
Everything that seems real
Will be false, a sham, a dream.
Baby, I can't sleep!
Your passion-filled moans echo in my ear,
Phantom caresses ripple across my skin
As I recall
Your sweet body
Yielding to me again and again.
And we stand at the door,
And we say our good-byes,
But I long to slide back
Between those big, pretty thighs.
Your love is so sweet.
Damn.
I don't want to leave
And baby...*sweet baby*,
I can...not...sleep.

"That's what I'm talking about!" a woman yelled.

The crowd's applause filled his ears. Lucas took a bow and exited the stage. When he approached the table, Ivy came to her feet. They moved toward each other at the same time, the rest of the world blocked out. He ignored the hands slapping him on the back and didn't even see Trenton and Alannah anymore. He only had eyes for Ivy, and no one else existed except the two of them. He lifted her off the floor in a tight squeeze.

"I meant every word I said, princess," he said, his voice thick. He never wanted to let her go. Never wanted to come down off this high.

"I love you," Ivy whispered in his ear. "And you are so getting laid again."

He laughed into her neck and then planted a kiss on her soft lips.

CHAPTER TWENTY-SIX

"What are you smiling about?"

Ivy looked up from her reports to see Cynthia standing in her office. She hadn't even heard her open the door and come in.

"Who me?" she asked.

"Yes, you. There's no one else in here." Cynthia placed more reports on her desk.

"Oh, I guess I'm just happy to be alive."

Cynthia raised a skeptical eyebrow. "Really? Or is it because Katie's father just left after being here for a couple of weeks?"

After the time he spent with her and Katie, Lucas had left for an engagement in New York. That trip had lasted a few days. Then he'd flown to Virginia for a business conference for influential men in media. Then it was back to Atlanta for a workshop, then down to Miami for a series of lectures on sex and the single woman.

But then he'd returned during the week of Christmas.

"Maybe," Ivy said. She bit her lip to keep from grinning outright.

Per tradition, Katie had traveled to Texas with Constance to spend the holidays with her great-grandparents. Cyrus Senior's death had taken place around this time of year and ever since her husband's death, Constance avoided the holidays in Seattle. She preferred to go to Texas and see her parents who were getting on in age and didn't travel as much as they used to.

Ivy and Lucas had flown down to join them for the twenty-third through the twenty-sixth, but otherwise they'd spent their days in Seattle. Lucas spoiled her the whole time. Not so much with material things, but with affection and thoughtfulness. He took her on dates and surprised her from time to time.

"I like to keep you on your toes," he'd said. She'd loved all the trouble he went through to make each date special.

One night he called her at work and told her when she came home that she would need to get dressed up. She arrived to finding him looking sharp in a tux, and he'd laid out the outfit he thought she should wear. They ended up at the Seattle Symphony. He'd bought tickets to the performance of Vivaldi's *Four Seasons* and hadn't said a word. She'd been surprised and happy, and she'd held onto his arm the entire night, enthralled by the sounds of the stringed instruments—the cello, the viola, and the violin.

There were also the more intimate times, when they were all alone and he catered to her. As recently as Saturday night, after a bout of explosive sex, they'd rolled out of bed and he'd offered to fix her a snack. She'd sat on the counter in a pair of white panties and his white undershirt and Lucas had been shirtless. His dark brown skin had gleamed under the lights, and his muscles had rippled with each movement as he worked on one of his princess sandwiches.

He worked diligently at the task, frowning so hard she had to hide a smile at his expense. She knew he wanted to make it perfect for her. He couldn't have been more concerned about quality if he were the pastry chef at a fine dining restaurant preparing the pièce de résistance to an elegant meal. A delicate chocolate soufflé perhaps, or a towering croquembouche.

He watched the stove like a hawk and made sure the bread didn't toast a shade browner than she liked. Then he flipped it over, chocolate oozing over the sides. When he finally finished, he cut off the edges and presented the sandwich on a plate. It had been delicious, of course. For some reason, the sandwich tasted better when he made it.

They'd chatted and then he'd said something funny, which made her laugh, hard. She'd covered her mouth and he'd pulled away her hand.

"Why do you do that?" he'd asked.

"Because I sound like a banshee."

"Hm, you're right."

She'd punched his shoulder.

"Don't hurt your hand," he'd said, his usual response whenever she hit him.

He'd stepped between her legs and rested his hands on either side of her thighs. "I love your laugh. Stop stifling it."

Then he'd bent his head and licked the chocolate that had dripped onto her thigh.

Right now, Cynthia cocked her head at Ivy. "There you go, smiling again. It's good to see you like this. He's good for you."

Ivy put down the pen and rested her chin in her hand. "He's gone now, though. He flew to Hawaii for a promotional thing there. Then he goes back to Atlanta because he starts teaching English at Mercer University this spring."

"When's he coming back?"

"I don't know." She'd grown accustomed to having him around during those couple of weeks. She wanted him in Seattle all the time. She wondered if that would ever be a possibility. "We didn't really get a chance to talk about it, but I know he'll be busy for a while."

"I have a feeling he's going to start racking up even more frequent flyer miles."

Ivy nodded. She'd offered once to send their private jet to pick him up—even if it was only for one night—but he'd balked at the idea.

"You're not sending your jet to pick me up like I'm your boy toy," he said, his expression making it clear that he thought she was crazy for suggesting it.

"But it would be more convenient for you, and I don't mind," she insisted. "What's the big deal?"

"The big deal is, I'm a man, and I'm not having my woman send a plane to pick me up like I'm a piece of tail. No, thanks. I'll catch my own flights and I'll come when I can."

She'd been disappointed by his response, but Lucas lived by his own set of man rules, and she'd have to adjust. She did, however, toy with the idea of flying to him. Maybe she could surprise him one night. Or one weekend when he couldn't get away, she and Katie could fly down and visit him in Georgia.

"Just a reminder that I'm leaving early for my doctor's appointment," Cynthia said on her way out the door. "I ordered your lunch and they're bringing it up at noon. I'll have Abigail bring it back for you."

Ivy waved her acknowledgement and went back to work. With Cynthia gone, the staff had strict instructions not to disturb her. She had a mountain of tasks to get done, which was much harder with thoughts of Lucas running around in her head.

****

Ivy reviewed the numbers for the fifth time. She wasn't getting anywhere. She turned to the window and tried to force her thoughts in order.

With a bang that made her jump, Abigail from reception burst into her office. Abigail never left her post and never burst in anywhere. The wild expression on her face forced Ivy to her feet.

"What is it?"

"Ms. Johnson, I'm so sorry. The phone's been ringing off the hook. Katie's school called."

Fear twisted in Ivy's belly, and she placed her hands on the desk to keep the influx of sheer panic from knocking her to her knees.

"What happened?"

"Reporters, ma'am. The administration said they've been calling the school, and they've been calling here, too. They have questions about Lucas Baylor and want to know if it's true that he's Katie's biological father."

Once she recovered from the initial shock of Abigail's words, Ivy catapulted into action. She had to get to her daughter. If the press already knew where she went to school, it was only a matter of time before they showed up there.

"Call my driver and tell him to meet me in executive parking," she said, grabbing her purse. She hustled down the hallway with Abigail hot on her tail. "Tell my brothers what's going on."

By the time she took the executive elevator downstairs, Lloyd was already waiting for her. On the ride to the school, she started nibbling on the nail of her index finger and then stopped. She couldn't remember the last time she'd bitten her nails.

Yes, she could. In school, after "the incident."

"Hurry," she murmured to herself. It never failed that when she was in a hurry, the traffic crawled along at a turtle's pace.

The car climbed the hill toward the front of the school and she stared out the window in distraction. A few children chased each other on the grass, and others sat bent over books, getting in their homework as they waited for their parents' arrival.

"Ma'am."

She looked up at the edge in Lloyd's voice and saw what he did.

Sitting forward, she stared in disbelief. A news van was parked nearby and reporters were stationed at the front of the school, right outside the main building. Paparazzi and cameramen rounded out the group. The principal argued with them, waving her arms wildly in an effort to get them off the property, but they showed no indication they planned to leave.

Ivy's heart plummeted. "No," she whispered. No way she could sneak Katie past that group. Not through the front, anyway. Maybe she could through the back, but how would she get the message to her daughter?

Children poured out of the main building, their faces bright with excitement at the end of the school day. She caught sight of Katie in the middle of two of her friends, the smallest of the three of them. She looked so fragile and innocent in that moment. Whatever they were discussing was very funny, because the girls were huddled in a tight group, giggling at their childish jokes.

Maybe they won't know who she is, Ivy thought desperately, her heart thumping restlessly, her body burning up with fear.

No such luck. One of the reporters spotted her right away, and they all rushed forward like a flock of geese following their leader. They yelled her name, cameras flashing, microphones extended. Katie and her friends froze.

"Katie!" Ivy screamed.

Seized by panic, Ivy fumbled for the door handle, desperate to get to her little girl and protect her from the mob that descended on her.

"Ma'am!" Lloyd's voice cracked as sharp as a whip, snapping her out of her frantic state. "Stay here." He spoke calmly but firmly.

She knew she should let him do his job, but it took a grand effort to remain still.

"Hurry!" she said, but he was already exiting the car. She lost sight of him as he barreled through the horde of reporters.

She felt sick to her stomach, in the same way she'd felt fourteen years ago. Only this time the nausea was much worse and coupled with the wrenching pain of helplessness. Because they were attacking the best part of her—her innocent daughter.

Only seconds passed, but the length of time seemed longer as she waited. Then the throng turned in her direction when Lloyd reappeared, holding Katie with one arm and her book bag in his hand. Her daughter hid her face in his chest, her shoulders folded as she clung tight to his neck.

Ivy pushed open the door and a barrage of questions accosted her.

"Ms. Johnson, who is Lucas Baylor?"

"Ms. Johnson, who is Katie's father?"

The second Lloyd deposited Katie into her arms, he slammed the door shut.

Cameras flashed and illuminated the interior of the vehicle, despite the tinted windows. Ivy crushed her daughter in her arms and turned her back to the mob.

"Mommy, Mommy, they're trying to kill me," Katie sobbed.

"No baby, they're not trying to kill you. It's okay. It's okay." Ivy cupped her head and rubbed her back.

The driver door slammed and her eyes met Lloyd's in the rear view mirror.

"Hang on." He honked the horn once and hit the accelerator. He didn't bother to wait for the reporters to move out of the way. He seemed intent on running over them like bowling pins, but they wisely scattered.

On Ivy's lap, Katie's small body trembled like someone with muscle spasms. Her daughter's tears wet her neck.

"What did I do?" Katie cried.

"Shh," Ivy whispered, holding her tighter. "You didn't do anything, munchkin." She kissed her damp cheek and rocked her. "You didn't do anything wrong."

****

After the afternoon's chaos, the silence in the condo was golden. Ivy had turned the lights down low and left the room with only a faint yellow glow from the ones in the buildings on the other side of the window. She had been sitting in the near darkness for a long time with the phones turned off, just thinking.

Her daughter straddled her lap and lay asleep against her chest, breathing evenly. It had taken a solid two hours of constant reassurances to convince Katie no one wanted to hurt her and they had only yelled at her because they wanted her attention—not because they were mad.

She looked up at a knock on the door and right after, it clicked open. Cyrus appeared first with Trenton right behind him. They both wore unbuttoned dark trenches over their suits. Their footfalls touched quietly on the hardwood.

Cyrus looked down at her and Katie, silently observant. "How is she?" he asked after a moment.

"Could be better." Ivy tried to smile, but she couldn't, and neither of her brothers looked in the mood to smile anyway.

Cyrus heaved a sigh. "I know you don't want to hear this, but you have to consider..." He trailed off when she glared at him. She knew where he was going before he said the words. "I know you don't want to think your boyfriend did this, but you can't ignore the coincidence of the story coming out not long after your involvement with him started. I've already done some digging and found out someone sold the story about Katie's paternity, which has opened up questions about Winston's sexuality again. Senator Somerset and his wife have been hounded by the press. This person, whoever they are, sold pictures from Lucas and Katie's date night."

"You have absolutely no reason to think it's Lucas. One of the parents from the dance could have done it."

"Ivy," Cyrus said patiently, "his name and image are all over the news and they're talking about his book. It's great publicity for him. Don't let your feelings for him cloud your judgment." The unspoken word "again" hung heavy in the air. "You have to recognize—"

"No!" Ivy said. Katie stirred in her arms and Ivy stroked her back to settle her down. She lowered her voice. "No. He wouldn't go to the tabloids. He wouldn't do that to Katie. He wouldn't do that to us."

"I hope you're right," Trenton said. He wasn't as cynical as Cyrus, but he obviously had doubts about Lucas, too.

"If that's why the two of you came, you can leave now."

"We came because Mother sent us to get you," Cyrus said.

She understood why her mother had sent for them. They would be better off at the family mansion, securely locked away behind the gate. It was only a matter of time before reporters showed up at the hotel, pretending to be guests in the lobby or lurking in their cars in the underground parking garage, waiting to pounce at the sight of her and her daughter.

"Trent," Cyrus said, his voice indicating he was in command mode, "get in touch with Four Seasons management and find out the best way for us to get out of here. Take your Range Rover to whatever entrance they suggest. I don't want to take any chances going out the normal exits. They may have found Ivy's residence by now and could be lying in wait. Tell Mother we've got Ivy and Katie and will be there in less than an hour."

"I'm on it." Trenton walked out with the phone to his ear.

Cyrus looked at her. "Whoever did this," he said cautiously, "we're going to make them pay."

She wanted the guilty party to pay, too. They'd shared photos of her child and exposed her to the world long before Ivy was ready for her to be a public figure. Kids should be off limits, but in today's media culture, that was no longer the case. Paparazzi followed children of celebrities and other notable people all the time. She didn't want that for Katie. The time would soon come when her every action would be under a microscope, and they'd have to train her on how to handle the media. But it wasn't time yet.

She gnawed her bottom lip and reflected on Cyrus's words. Had she been wrong about Lucas? Could she have fallen for another ruse that exposed her, her family, and even the Somersets to unwanted scrutiny? What person would do this to them? Her thoughts shied away from Lucas being the guilty party.

"We didn't exactly try to hide Lucas and Katie's relationship, and everything that's been said—for the most part—is true." Her gaze met her brother's. "Just find out who sold the story." And please don't let it be Lucas.

"I will." Cyrus sat down beside her. "We need to get the two of you out of here. I'll take her. Get together your clothes and everything you'll both need."

Katie protested mildly as they shifted her from one lap to the other, but she quickly settled down in her uncle's arms.

Ivy paused on her way out of the room. "Did Mother say how long she wanted us to stay?"

Cyrus glanced at her. "As long as you need to."

****

"Come on, answer the phone. Answer the phone."

The call went to Ivy's voice mail, and Lucas hung up in frustration. He let out an angry yell and almost crushed the device in his fury. He missed the days when he could slam a phone into its cradle.

He'd lost track of how many times he'd called Ivy, and she hadn't answered yet. He figured she had her phone turned off to avoid unwanted calls, but he worried she might think he had something to do with the story that broke.

He dropped into the chair at the desk in his hotel room and stared in frustration at the computer screen. The travel options to Seattle were depressing. With no available outgoing flights until tomorrow afternoon, he was about ready to swim from Hawaii to the mainland.

The phone rang and he almost jumped out of his skin. He lunged for it where it lay on a side table, but it wasn't Ivy. It was Brenda. She'd texted him earlier today when the news hit.

"Well?" he asked. He'd charged her with getting him out of his obligation at the resort.

"Lucas, they're not happy about this, particularly in light of what's recently happened."

The hosts wanted him to stay put at the resort and finish the week with the other speakers. The scandal about him and the heiress to the Johnson fortune made him an overnight celebrity, and having him at the week long couple's retreat had turned out to be an unexpected coup they wanted to milk for publicity.

"I don't care, Brenda."

He suspected she wasn't working as hard as she could. When she'd called him, she'd been way too excited about the press coverage and told him that bad publicity was better than no publicity at all. To which he'd replied she only said that because it wasn't her life, and by the way, she was out of her damn mind.

"At least consider waiting until the end of the week," Brenda said. "You can talk to Ivy and Katie on the phone, can't you?"

"She won't answer the phone," Lucas explained with barely contained impatience. He didn't go into further detail about his concern that Ivy might think he had something to do with the leak. "And frankly, I don't want to be here while they're going through this mess."

He couldn't get the picture of Ivy's driver, Lloyd, carrying his daughter through a throng of reporters and photographers out of his head. It made him sick to his stomach and it made him angry. She was just a kid. What was wrong with those people?

"I'll do the best I can," Brenda said. "But—"

"No buts, Brenda. Figure it out. You've done it before. Whether you get me out of this or not, I'm on a flight to Seattle tomorrow. I need to get to my daughter and my w—" He'd almost said wife, because that's how he thought of her now—with permanence, part of his future. Katie was his daughter, Ivy was his wife, *they* were his family.

"I need to get to my daughter and her mother," he said. "I need them to know that I didn't have any part in this, and I'm not some asshole who used them for publicity and violated their trust. That's not me. I'm not that guy. My job is to protect them and keep them safe. Because I'm a goddamn dragon slayer."

Chapter Twenty-seven

Numb, Ivy sat in her mother's sitting room listening to the family spokesperson, Hudson Lynch, run through scenarios. Hudson paced as his assistant took notes, and her mother nodded or shook her head depending on her agreement or disagreement with his ideas.

More details about her relationship with Winston had trickled into the media overnight. They liberally bandied about words such as "Full Moon cover up." One of Winston's exes had already surfaced to corroborate the rumors that Ivy and Winston had had a fake marriage. Some journalists even charged them with making a mockery of marriage.

Out on the campaign trail, reporters questioned Senator Somerset's integrity. Opponents on the left and right pointed out his hypocrisy and called for him to refrain from running for office. According to them, if he could force his son into a fake marriage to win an election, what wouldn't he do?

"Ivy?" Her gaze shifted to her mother, whose eyes were filled with concern. "What do you think?"

"I'm sorry, Mother, I wasn't paying attention," she admitted. She made a decision right then, based on an idea that had taken root in her mind. She addressed Hudson. "I'm glad you're here, but I don't want to do a press release or send out a finely crafted message to your media contacts. I want to face the press myself."

"With all due respect, Ms. Johnson, you should let us handle this." Hudson looked at Ivy's mother for concurrence.

"They're going to try to rip you to shreds, dear." Constance looked her steadily in the eyes. "Are you sure?"

"They've already started," Hudson said. "Some of the headlines make reference to what happened fourteen years ago. The name-calling, it's—it's not pretty..." His voice trailed off politely rather than repeat the headlines.

Not that Ivy hadn't seen them herself. She knew the names they called her and that made her more determined than ever to face her detractors.

She kept her eyes on her mother, because she, more than anyone, had to be convinced. "Mother, I can handle it."

"I don't advise—"

Constance lifted her hand and Hudson fell silent. "What were you thinking?" she asked Ivy.

"A press conference," Ivy answered. The thought had come to her out of the blue. "Where I could explain what happened—just enough details to satisfy their curiosity, but more than that. I want to look them in the eyes and tell them to leave my daughter alone. That's the most important part. I don't want them hounding her."

Constance took her hand and squeezed it between her thinner fingers. "I believe you're doing the right thing. The more you hide, the more they'll seek their own truth. You have to be the one to craft the message." She turned to Hudson. "You heard my daughter. She's going to speak for herself. Draft a statement right away for her approval."

Hudson didn't look pleased and opened his mouth to speak again, but the sound of raised voices at the front of the house interrupted him. Ivy's heart tripped over the next beat. One of those voices sounded like Lucas.

"I'll be right back."

She rushed out on unsteady legs to see Trenton and Lucas up in each other's face, practically nose to nose. Trenton had taken the day off and was dressed casually in a pair of jeans and T-shirt. Lucas wore a rumpled dress shirt and slacks. He looked like he'd slept in his clothes.

"What's going on?" Ivy asked.

They both turned in her direction. Lucas started toward her, but Trenton put a restraining hand on his shoulder. Lucas knocked it off and both men shoved each other.

"Stop it!" Ivy said. "Both of you."

"Say the word and he's out of here," Trenton said. His right hand curled into a fist.

"I didn't go to the tabloids, Ivy," Lucas said.

"It sure is coincidental that for eight years no one has known the truth, but you come into our lives and her business is all over the news."

Lucas's jaw clenched, the only indication he'd heard Trenton speak. He ignored her brother and spoke directly to her. "Somebody else went to the tabloids. Not me." He trapped her with his earnest gaze.

Ivy wanted to believe him. She'd tossed and turned all night, second-guessing herself and wondering if her brothers could have been right after all.

"How do you explain the photos?" she asked. That was the most damning evidence of all. Even if the release of the story could be deemed a coincidence, the press had photos of Katie and Lucas from the father and daughter dance. That's how the paparazzi had been able to identify her at school.

"I don't have an answer," Lucas said, "but I swear to you, I didn't give anyone pictures of me and Katie."

Trenton snorted in disgust.

"Trenton." Constance had entered the foyer without Ivy noticing. "Please join me in the sitting room."

After a short hesitation, Trenton sent one last scathing look at Lucas and walked away with his mother.

"How'd you get onto the property?" Ivy asked.

"I climbed the fence. It wasn't easy because I'm not as young as I used to be." His smile disappeared when she didn't smile back. "God, Ivy, you have to know I wouldn't do this. It's killing me that you're looking at me with such distrust."

She didn't know what to think. She hadn't thought him capable of such a betrayal, but the circumstantial evidence made him look like the guilty party. He certainly had plenty to gain from the publicity. In addition to selling the story, his book sales would probably skyrocket.

"I've been wrong before," she said, "and this media circus doesn't only affect me. It affects Katie, too. They terrified her, Lucas. She was shaking like a leaf in my arms because she thought they wanted to hurt her."

"Do you really think I'd be capable of doing this to our daughter?

To you? I would rather cut off my right arm than hurt either one of you. You and Katie mean the world to me." He swallowed hard. "I admit I didn't want a family at first, but I'm happier now than I've ever been, and it's because of the two of you. I wouldn't jeopardize that, and I wouldn't risk your happiness to make a few bucks."

He was saying all the right things.

"You have to believe me, Ivy. If I have to find out myself who did this to you—to us—I will. Don't shut me out."

He took one step toward her, and when she didn't move, he took another, then another, until he was standing right in front of her and she could smell his cologne. The familiar scent weakened her. The wall she'd erected for self-preservation crumbled, and she started shaking. That's when he pulled her into the security of his arms.

She'd had to be strong for Katie and put on a brave face for her family, but with Lucas she could just be.

"They're saying such awful things," she said, her voice quivering. Tears sprang to her eyes.

She'd stopped reading the headlines. They'd been too painful:

"Fourteen Years Later the Billionaire Heiress is at it Again"

"Sex, Lies, and Paternity Tests—A Day in the Life of Ivy Johnson"

"Who's Really the Daddy?" That particular article had gone so far as to suggest Lucas get a DNA test to confirm Katie's paternity.

"We'll get through this, you'll see," Lucas said. He massaged the back of her neck with his thumb.

She swiped at the tears on her cheeks. "I shouldn't have doubted you. I just…"

"It's okay. I'm here, and we'll be fine. Katie will be fine." He pressed soft kisses to her eyelids. She buried her face in his neck and soaked up the comforting warmth of his embrace.

Footsteps sounded on the tile, and Ivy turned to see Trenton coming toward them with his cell phone in hand. "I just talked to Cyrus. He knows who did it."

"Who?" Ivy asked.

"It was a woman."

"A woman?" Lucas asked sharply. Ivy looked at him. By the tone of his voice, he sounded almost as if he'd guessed who the culprit was.

"What woman?" Ivy asked.

"Your babysitter," Trenton answered. "Janelle sold you out."

CHAPTER TWENTY-EIGHT

The press conference went better than expected. Ivy and Lucas presented a united front to the media. They confirmed that he was indeed Katie's father and praised Winston's role in her life. At the end they asked the reporters and paparazzi to stay away from their daughter and her school.

Josiah Somerset also spoke and admitted he didn't understand his son's preferences, that he himself couldn't pretend that a lot of his friends were gay. Soft chuckles rippled through the crowd at his admission. He wrapped up by telling everyone, in a trembling voice that reflected his pain, that Winston was his only son, and his political and religious leanings didn't mean he loved him any less.

Ivy let the attorneys deal with Nanny Services on Call, the company she'd used to vet and hire Janelle. The young woman had signed a confidentiality agreement and violated it when she sold personal information to the tabloids.

She'd liked Janelle and was devastated to learn that she'd been the one to betray them. Ivy ransacked her brain to figure out if she'd mistreated Janelle in any way, trying to find an explanation for the young woman's actions, but she found none. The only conclusion she drew was that Janelle had been motivated by greed. Plain and simple.

****

Ivy heard Lucas enter the bedroom and looked up from a text she was writing to Trenton. "Is she okay?" she asked, referring to Katie. He'd tucked her in.

Lucas nodded. He dropped his jacket on the mattress. "Yes. Wasn't it you who told me kids are amazingly resilient?"

She smiled. "I believe so."

In truth, Katie had already recovered from the incident at her school. It helped having Lucas there the past few days. He showered her with attention and his presence had been a tremendous boost to her spirits.

He strolled over to the chaise lounge and sat down beside her.

Ivy finished her text and hit send. She cast a glance at him. "Are you all right?"

Could he be second-guessing getting involved with her? So much had happened. They'd spent the last few days at her mother's house and had agreed to let Hudson send a short statement to the media outlets since they'd already had a chance to tell their side of the story. Her brothers had come around, too. They'd both apologized to him and finally accepted he meant the family no harm.

"I'm all right." He cupped her face and stroked her cheek with his thumb.

"I hate that you were so exposed and had to have your life dissected in this way."

He shrugged. "I was already in the public eye to some degree, though not to this extent," he contended.

"You didn't sign up for this."

"Neither did you."

"I've had more practice dealing with this type of media scrutiny."

"I bet it doesn't get any easier." He stroked her hair back from her face. "Doesn't matter anyway. We're in this together, right?"

"Yes, we are," she agreed with a smile. "And I'm so glad you're here." She grasped his hand and pressed her lips to his palm.

"Me, too. I'm right where I want to be."

Her brow wrinkled. "Then what's wrong?"

Lucas took her hands in his. He frowned thoughtfully. "I hate being away from you and Katie. When things like this happen, I should be here."

"We'll work it out."

He took a deep breath and looked into her eyes. "I'm going to sell my condo. It's in a great location in Atlanta, and if I put it on the market this spring, it should sell by summer when I'm done teaching at Mercer. Then I could move up here."

Ivy's mouth fell open. "You're moving here? To Seattle?" Was this a dream?

His face lit up into one of his dazzling smiles. "Yes."

Ivy let out an excited squeal and tackled him, knocking him on to his back on the lounge. She showered his face with kisses.

He laughed. "I take it you're okay with that?" he asked.

She answered by cupping his face and planting a long, slow kiss on his lips.

He groaned and swelled against her hip. "Show me again how okay you are with my idea," he murmured. "I'm not sure I understand."

His hands slid down to her derriere and it was her turn to groan. She planted another kiss on him and traced his lips with the tip of her tongue.

"Better?" she asked.

"Better," he whispered.

He slapped her on the behind and she moaned. Biting her bottom lip, she stared down into his beautiful eyes. "You make me so happy," she whispered.

"You make *me* so happy," he said. "I love you so much, Ivy. I never want you to doubt how I feel about you ever again." He pulled her head down to his, burying his fingers in her hair, and tasted her mouth. His lips stroked gently across hers. "Let's go take a shower. And then I'm going to make love to you—not necessarily in that order."

She slid off of him, making sure to bump his hard-on as she did.

"Tease," he groaned.

In the bathroom they leisurely soaped each other's skin, and when they finished, Lucas ran his hands down her body, sloughing off the suds as if the water needed any help from him. Ivy lowered to her knees and slipped his erection between her lips, worshipping its length and girth with her mouth and tongue. She pulled back to the tip and hummed in the back of her throat, reveling in the fact that he had to hold onto the wall to keep from collapsing.

"You're killing me," he muttered.

He grabbed her hair, and his head fell back as he gave himself over to the moist suction of her mouth. But rather than let her suck him off, he pulled her to her feet. Standing behind her, he sandwiched her between his body and the wall.

With her cheek pressed against the cold tile, one large hand binding her wrists above her head and the other on her hip, he stroked into her from behind. Her breasts jostled from the impact, each thrust hard, but slow. He slid out, then back into her, inch by marvelous inch. He felt so good she didn't want him to stop.

He pinched her nipples between this thumb and forefinger, pulling the peaks taut and using them to shake her breasts. Heat, fierce and hot, pounded through her loins. She was so close, pushing back against his groin and lifting her hips to receive him.

"I love you," he whispered hotly in her ear. "I love you so damn much."

With one powerful pump, he speared her with the full length of his erection. A sharp cry fled her throat, and her hands curled into fists against the Italian tile. Her muscles contracted and pulsed around him. Muttering a hoarse oath into the wet hair flattened on her back, his body emptied into hers.

****

Outside the bedroom window, the lights from the buildings glowed like stars in a far away galaxy. Lucas stroked Ivy's silky hair and the line of her spine. Her skin was so soft, and her sweet, feminine smell filled his nostrils.

He couldn't sleep. He couldn't stop looking at her, and his mind raced with too many thoughts and plans.

Rather than continue to lay there wide awake, he eased out of Ivy's arms, careful not to wake her, and slipped on a pair of boxers. He lifted the phone from his pants pocket and took it with him out of the room. He walked past the media room and peeked in on Katie, and then he moved quietly down the hall to the living room where he settled on the sofa.

He dialed the number for his best friend, Roarke, who was back in Chile.

Roarke's friendly voice came on the line. "Hey man, how's it going?"

Lucas slouched in the chair. "Going all right. According to my publisher, *The Rules of Man* has a shot at hitting the New York Times Bestsellers List."

Not exactly the way he would have wanted to make the list. The story about Katie's paternity had garnered a lot of publicity for him. This in turn had made his blog more popular, and his book had seen a surge in sales.

Brenda had been ecstatic and wanted to book him for as many appearances as possible, but he'd asked her to cut back on the engagements. Doing all of that traveling had been tiring anyway, and now he had an even greater reason to cut back. He'd rather be here with Ivy and Katie whenever he had free days.

"New York Times?" Roarke said. "Get the hell outta here."

Lucas chuckled. "It hasn't happened yet. We'll know next week."

"I'm confident it'll happen for you."

"Thanks, man. Hey, I need to ask you a favor." He lowered his voice.

"Sure, anything."

"I want you to be my best man."

"You're engaged?"

Lucas laughed at the incredulity in his friend's voice. "Not yet. But soon enough, when I ask her."

"You sure she's going to say yes?" Roarke asked with a laugh.

"You got jokes. Yeah, I'm sure."

"Say the word and I'm there."

"Thanks. I knew I could count on you."

They talked for some time. Lucas gave him an update on what had happened over the past few days and Roarke relayed information on his work in Chile and his latest research.

"Lucas?" Ivy's voice came from behind him. He turned around to see her wearing his shirt. One button held together both sides, and her hair spilled onto her shoulders and down her back in a glorious, tousled mess. "You coming back to bed soon?"

"Roarke, I've got to go."

"Okay, I—"

Lucas hung up and tossed the phone onto the sofa.

Ivy smiled as he walked toward her. She looked like a girl from a pinup magazine, and he'd already grown hard with thoughts of what he would do to her once they went back to the bedroom.

"You missed your man?" he asked.

"Mhmm." She squealed when he hoisted her from the floor. Her legs locked around his waist.

"You're going to have to show me how much you missed me," he warned.

She giggled and nibbled on his ear. The touch of her teeth sent shivers of pleasure straight to his groin.

"I'm happy to oblige," she whispered.

That made him lengthen his strides and hurry down the hall. When they arrived in the bedroom, he laid her on the bed and brushed his lips over hers. She moaned softly and kissed him back.

He looked down into her lovely face. He had to be the luckiest man in the world. With a wicked smile, he said, "Okay princess, let me see what you've got."

The End

MORE STORIES BY DELANEY DIAMOND

Hot Latin Men series
The Arrangement
Fight for Love
Private Acts
Second Chances
Hot Latin Men: Vol. I (print anthology)
Hot Latin Men: Vol. II (print anthology)

Hawthorne Family series
The Temptation of a Good Man
A Hard Man to Love
Here Comes Trouble
For Better or Worse
Hawthorne Family Series: Vol. I (print anthology)
Hawthorne Family Series: Vol. II (print anthology)

Love Unexpected series
The Blind Date
The Wrong Man

Johnson Family series
Unforgettable
Perfect (fall 2014)
Just Friends (spring 2015)

Bailar series (sweet/clean romance)
Worth Waiting For

Short Stories
Subordinate Position
The Ultimate Merger

Free Stories
www.delaneydiamond.com

ABOUT THE AUTHOR

Delaney Diamond is the USA Today Bestselling Author of sweet, sensual, passionate romance novels. Originally from the U.S. Virgin Islands, she now lives in Atlanta, Georgia. She reads romance novels, mysteries, thrillers, and a fair amount of nonfiction. When she's not busy reading or writing, she's in the kitchen trying out new recipes, dining at one of her favorite restaurants, or traveling to an interesting locale. She speaks fluent conversational French and can get by in Spanish.

Enjoy free reads and the first chapter of all her novels on her website. Join her e-mail mailing list to get sneak peeks, notices of sale prices, and find out about new releases.

www.delaneydiamond.com
www.facebook.com/DelaneyDiamond

CPSIA information can be obtained
at www.ICGtesting.com
Printed in the USA
FSOW02n2138140616
21557FS